THE LAST DAYS
OF THE ROMANOVS

THE LAST DAYS
OF THE ROMANOVS

MICHAEL MULLEN

POOLBEG

Published in 1995
by Poolbeg Press Ltd
123 Baldoyle Industrial Estate
Dublin 13, Ireland

© Michael Mullen 1995

The moral right of the authors has been asserted.

A catalogue record for this book is available from the British Library.

ISBN 1 85371 520 4

Cover illustrations by Michael Mascaro
Cover design by Poolbeg Group Services Ltd
Set by Poolbeg Group Services Ltd in Garamond 11/13
Printed by The Guernsey Press Ltd,
Vale, Guernsey, Channel Islands.

A NOTE ON THE AUTHOR

Michael Mullen lives in Castlebar, Co Mayo. He is the author of many successful historical novels for adults and children, including the bestseller *The Hungry Land*.

CHAPTER 1

The snow lay deep about the Alexander Palace. A winter haze encircled the barks of the silver birch trees which stood about the grounds. No sound broke the stillness. It was an enchanted scene.

For four hundred years the Romanovs had ruled Russia. Their empire stretched from the borders of Poland to the Sea of Japan. Soon their world would come crashing down. Time was running out.

In the city of Saint Petersburg, twenty miles to the north, discontent was deep. The ravages of the First World War were everywhere. Young men, their eyes blinded by shrapnel, stared blankly into space. The maimed cried out for food. People complained of hunger.

On the battle front the carnage was horrific. The dead were buried in nameless graves and the wounded carried home in trains and carts.

Mother Russia was in agony.

The doors of the Alexander Palace opened. Nicholas II, Tsar of all the Russias, walked down the steps and made his way through the snow. His face was creased with worry. He passed through paths choked by weeds and reached the birch woods. Here he could find some peace; he always found peace in the woods.

The burden of empire was too great for him. He should never have been crowned Tsar at all. He was a lonely figure in the snow-filled woods. Soldiers watched the solitary figure. It was their business to protect him. Dressed in great coats against the cold, they kept out of sight. The soldiers belonged to a crack Cossack regiment. They would lay down their lives for Nicholas II.

Nicholas passed between the trees. His boots crunched in the thick snow and he could see his breath in the sharp air. He stood and looked about him. Everywhere the snow lay pure and unfranked. Then he thought of the soldiers at the battle fronts. In his mind's eye he could see snow churned into slush and stained with blood. He covered his eyes with his hands and cried out. When he opened them again, the woods were calm and empty. A voice called to him. He recognised it as belonging to Tatiana, the tallest of his daughters. Her hair was auburn and her eyes deep grey and she carried herself the way a princess should.

"Papa! Papa!" she called.

He called back and waited for her to catch up. His heart lightened at the sight of so beautiful a girl. Some day she would marry into one of the Royal families of Europe. Perhaps all four of his daughters would cement relationships with the Royal houses of Europe and help to bring a lasting peace.

At last Tatania caught up with him. She was dressed in a long fur coat.

"How beautiful it is in the woods Papa," she said. "You always go to the woods when you are troubled."

"You know me so well," he smiled. She linked his arm and they moved further into the birch woods. They did not talk for some time. They were happy in each other's company and wished to prolong the delicious moment.

"Today I thought of our summers in the Crimea," she said.

"We will go there again when this war is over. We will walk through the vineyards and the small villages close to Yalta. At night time we shall leave all the windows of the palace open and let the perfumed air pass through the rooms," he promised her.

Only the crunching sound of their boots on the snow broke the silence as they walked deeper and deeper into the woods.

"It is time to return. There is always some urgent business to attend to. You look tired. You spend too much time at the hospital," he told his daughter as they turned around and began to walk back towards the palace.

"The soldiers need us, Papa. Today we received more wounded from the Front. It was terrible. We cleaned their wounds and bandaged them as best we could. Mama spent two hours in the operating theatre with the surgeons."

"I worry for her health. This war has taken its toll on all our lives."

"Except Anastasia. She plays billiards with the soldiers. She is a such a tomboy!"

"Anastasia was born to entertain. Leave her to her ways. She keeps us happy and we need someone to make us happy during these difficult times."

Tatiana looked at her father. Three years of war had made him old. His face was thin and pale, wrinkles now scored his cheeks and the whites of his eyes were tinged with yellow. She felt that his mind was strained under the burden of war.

They continued to walk through the trees towards the palace.

The Royal estate, Tsarskoe Selo, was an enchanted place. Cossack horsemen in scarlet tunics and black fur hats patrolled its margin. From the tall windows of the palace the Tsar could look down on terraces and gardens.

Now the two figures walked across the snow towards the palace entrance. They moved up the steps and entered the great foyer. Tsarskoe Selo was a palace of long halls and rooms furnished in marble, mahogany, gold, crystal, velvet and silk. Great chandeliers fragmented the light into a thousand rays. They passed across oriental rugs to the library where large maps lay opened on the table.

"Tell me about the war, Papa," Tatiana said.

"It is too terrible. Too terrible," her father replied.

With a thin cane he outlined the Russian positions on one of the maps which lay open on the table. Everywhere the armies had been beaten back.

"The slaughter is terrible. We were ill prepared for such a war. I was badly advised. My ministers are corrupt men."

"Can you not make peace with the German Kaiser? You are related to him."

"It has gone too far. The time to sue for peace has passed. Now every country has been drawn into this struggle."

"When will it end?"

"Soon I hope," Nicholas said in a weary voice.

"Leave me now, Tatiana. There is much to consider. I wish to be alone with my thoughts."

She left the room. Before she closed the door, she looked at her father's expression. The smile had left his face and he looked dejected.

She passed along the corridor. Her mind was filled with anxiety. She could sense that they were living through one of the most dangerous moments in the history of Russia. She had listened to the conversations of the officers in the hospital wards. The people were turning away from her father. This disaster was being blamed on him.

The Russia which Tatiana loved, with its vast steppes to the east, now snow-bound, and the mountainous regions to the south, was in turmoil. The people lit their candles before ancient icons, black with the rime of centuries. Still, no miracle happened. Men continued to die on the Front.

She arrived at the door of her brother's room. Life in the palace revolved about Alexei. He would be the future Tsar. As always, his room was guarded against assassins.

Tatiana knocked on the door and entered.

Alexei lay on a soft bed which would not bruise his flesh. Sitting beside him on a satin armchair, his mother Alexandra kept vigil. Now forty-six years of age, she still looked beautiful. She had been born in Darmstadt, a medieval German city with narrow cobble-stone streets and steeply roofed houses. Like many German princesses who had married into the Russian Royal family, she had become truly Russian and loved the vast sprawling empire. Her grandmother had been Queen Victoria and she was related through blood to most of the Royal families of Europe. Queen Victoria, at first, did not agree with her grand-daughter marrying Nicholas. She felt that the Russian Empire was a dangerous place for a young Empress. But Nicholas and Alexandra loved each other and the marriage had been a great success. Alexandra was a deeply religious woman who felt that there was sadness beneath all beauty. Part of her mind was practical and part of it was mystical.

Alexei was asleep. Tatiana looked at his face. It was without pain. He was the youngest of the family and they all took a deep interest in his well-being.

Very few knew the secret. It had been kept hidden from the people since his birth. Alexei was now thirteen years of age, fair-skinned and handsome. Tatiana could hardly believe, as she watched her brother sleeping, that Alexei, heir to all the Russias, was a haemophiliac.

On the day he was born, the guns of Saint Petersburg had boomed out in joy. An heir had been born to the Russian throne.

Six weeks later the baby began to bleed.

As the child learned to crawl, it was noted that when he bumped into his crib, dark swellings appeared beneath his skin. As he grew older, his blood would not clot.

"Is he asleep, mother?"

"Yes."

"I will watch him for a while. You take a rest."

"How is father?"

"He is sad. Oh, will this war ever end? It is a great burden."

"I do not know. He is under a terrible strain. His enemies plot against him."

"Go and rest, Mother. You cannot always stay by his bed. You are tired. I will sit with Alexei."

"If the holy monk Rasputin were alive, he would guide us," the Tsarina said. "I trusted him. When they killed him they killed Russia."

Rasputin had been a strange visitor to the palace. Long-haired and wild-looking, a holy man from Siberia, he had the strange ability to heal Alexei. He had been assassinated by Prince Youssoupoff, his body thrown into the Neva river which ran through Saint Petersburg.

Rasputin had been a mysterious character. His fiery eyes could pierce the secrets of the mind; his hands carried a healing power. He seemed to come from nowhere in the wide spaces of Siberia and had taken control of the court with his strange gift of healing and his second sight.

Now he was dead. But a year earlier he had free access to the palace and to state secrets. He had controlled the power behind the throne.

The Tsarina left the room and Tatiana sat beside her brother. He was breathing deeply. She studied his fine skin and his good looks. Some day he would be the Tsar of Russia.

She picked up a book and flicked through the pages.

Outside it grew dark. Snow fell on Tsarskoe Selo. The lights went on in the great palace. Tatiana went to the window and looked out. Huge snowflakes fell softly on the parks and lawns. They were changed to gold by the lights.

As she gazed down she noted somebody arriving in a troika. It pulled up and a figure got out. She did not recognise him. He was dressed in a great fur coat and wore a sable hat. He passed up the steps.

So, another visitor to see her father. They came at all hours of the day and night.

Looking out into the darkness, Tatiana recalled the happy days the family had spent together at Tsarskoe Selo and in the Crimea. Her sisters, Anastasia, Maria and Olga, had filled the palace corridors with laughter. She thought of the Crimea and the Livadia Palace which stood above the sea. Behind it lay the great barrier of mountains which caught the early morning light. The gardens were filled with exotic flowers and she often played with her sisters amongst the pathways.

Tatiana went to the library shelf and took down an album of photographs and began to study them.

A photograph of the family taken at Saint Petersburg in 1904 caught her attention. She could barely remember the occasion. They were all dressed in similar outfits. It must have been summer time. The dresses were light and edged with lace.

There was a photograph of her father and the girls paddling on the coast of Finland. Her father looked like a peasant. He always dressed in simple clothes.

1909 was celebrated with a photograph of Alexei in an automobile, taken at Tsarskoe Selo. It was a glistening vehicle with deep plush seats and a roof which could be drawn forward when it rained. He was dressed like a young officer. Alexei was very fond of military uniforms.

There were several photographs taken in 1911. She noted that they had all grown. They were never apart and had always shared their secrets.

By 1913 the Romanov daughters appeared to have become young women. They dressed in the fashion of the day and had moved into society.

Their life changed in 1914. They moved about the empire meeting officers from the army; they became aware of how vast Russia was.

By 1915 they seemed so mature. They posed for a photograph in nurses' uniforms with their mother. They had been well trained and took pride in their work at the hospital on the Tsarskoe Selo estate.

As Tatiana leafed through the photographs, her sister Olga entered the room. She was almost two years older than Tatiana.

"Is Alexei asleep?" she whispered.

"Yes."

"Good. I wish to talk to you. I believe that Father intends to return to the battle front."

"But he should remain here," Tatiana replied. "Does he not know that Saint Petersburg is on the brink of revolution? I talk with the officers. These are most dangerous times: one spark and the people might rise against us. He is needed here. His presence alone could quell a rebellion. If he leaves for the war front, then he is making a grave mistake."

"The burden upon him is weighing him down."

"He should be more decisive. The whole government is inefficient. He should show himself in Saint Petersburg. People love him. They regard him as their father."

Tatiana spoke in a serious manner. She understood the political position better than her sisters.

"I heard him talking with mother," Olga said in whispered tones.

"What did they say?"

"I don't know, but I have premonitions. I often have them when I kneel before the icons. We seem to be making an endless journey to the east. It is always the east. And then I hear revolver fire and blood on the snow. It is terrible."

Tatiana was silenced by Olga's admission. She often had premonitions, and they were accurate.

"Everyone feels so helpless. I have seen the ambassadors and ministers come and go during the last months. Papa should sack the members of his government. Many of them are corrupt. It is time for a change!"

"He is too weak to change; the burden has become too great for him."

Alexei awoke.

"Is it morning?" he asked, rubbing his eyes.

"No, Alexei," Tatiana replied.

"Then I have slept only a short time. I had a dream. I was master of a circus and I had trained all the animals and received great applause."

"Perhaps you would prefer to become a circus master than Tsar," Olga suggested.

"It would be so much more interesting," Alexei responded.

Tatiana placed the photograph album on the bed and they examined them together. Outside the snow continued to fall on the great woods and flat lands and on Saint Petersburg. As they studied the photographs, they could not know that the empire was about to collapse.

CHAPTER 2

Saint Petersburg was a beautiful city. Only Paris equalled it in splendour. The Nevsky Prospect ran through the centre, leading to the Winter Palace and the Neva river. The elegant shops contained goods from all over the world. The most modern and expensive cars brushed past troikas and sledges. There was always frenetic movement on the Prospect.

Along the canals, walled with pink granite, stood the palaces of the Russian princes; their vast estates lay scattered across the Russian Empire. These palaces were laden with treasures and during the winter season echoed with the sound of music and laughing voices. Their fortunes were limitless.

Two hundred thousand men had died in order to raise this city on mud flats. Slaves and prisoners, they worked in mud, died in mud and were buried in mud. Saint Petersburg was sometimes known as "the city of the bones".

The great cathedral of Saint Isaac's equalled Saint Peter's of Rome in magnificence. At the end of the Prospect and a little to the left stood a great square and before it the Winter Palace with its vast treasures.

Beyond the Winter Palace stood the river Neva. It flowed into the Gulf of Finland; in winter it froze over with thick ice. Beyond the river stood the formidable fortress of Saint Peter and Paul's.

To the north of the city, where the great factory chimneys belched out smoke, things were very different. There the workers lived in a warren of small houses that offered little protection against the cold.

Vasily was fourteen years old and tall for his age. All that winter he had been cold. His mother worked in the cloth mill. Every morning, before the crack of dawn, she woke like all the other women who worked in the mills. They stirred in the darkness calling out to each other's cabins.

Ice formed on the timber cabins' inner walls. The workers were hungry. They had been cold and hungry all winter. Several small children had died from malnutrition. Vasily watched them waste away. Their tiny bodies had been carried to the graveyard, wrapped in rags. There, frozen earth was broken with pickaxes and they were placed in shallow graves. The families could not even afford wooden coffins. Timber was too precious.

Vasily's house consisted of two rooms. The bedroom was divided in half by a curtain which was drawn at night time.

"The poor have short, sad lives," his mother had told him often.

Life had seemed bleak since the war began. The war was to the west of Saint Petersburg, far away. Vasily had watched fine armies march westwards to the music of military bands and had seen the broken remnants return on carts and cattle wagons, limbs missing and wounds wrapped in soiled bandages.

His mother stirred in the bed.

"See if the lanterns are lit in the other houses," she called to him.

He left his bed and looked out. Yes the dark streets were coming to life.

"Yes, Mother. I will prepare the stove."

"Don't use more fuel than you need to."

Vasily broke some kindling and set them in the grate lighting them with a match. Then he placed some of the timber sticks he had found in the woods on top of the flames. When they were glowing, he set small lumps of coal upon them. Soon the small cabin was warm.

"I wish that I could take your place in the factory, Mother," he said when she emerged from the room.

"You are too young. Besides I wish you to continue your education. You are a bright lad; you can read and write. It is a wonderful gift, one which will serve you well. You will break free of this terrible place."

Vasily heated some gruel for his mother in a pot on the stove; she ate the sticky mess.

"Here is some bread," he told her.

It was bread with a white heart which he had stolen from a confectioner's shop on the Nevsky Prospect and had saved to surprise his mother with.

Vasily's mother looked at it in wonder. Then with her long fingers she broke a morsel off and ate it.

"It is sweet like honey," she said. "Fit for the Tsar's table."

He winced when he heard her mention the Tsar. He hated Nicholas. The Tsar was the cause of all the troubles which now beset them.

"Perhaps this evening I will have another tasty surprise for you," he said when she had eaten the bread.

She would have to work all day without a meal and in the evening she would be exhausted. The women at the factory were only beasts of burden who worked long hours and kept silent about their condition.

She bore her fate with resignation. Before she left, she knelt before the icons and prayed to the saints to protect her during the day.

Then in the dark she left the house and joined the others. Vasily could hear them talking as they made their way down the narrow lane between the houses.

Vasily knew that he was master of his own fate. His father had died early in the war and his death had hardened Vasily's heart. He took the revolutionary paper he had found crumpled on the Nevsky Prospect. He smoothed it out on the rough table as if it were a precious object. Then by lantern light he began to read it slowly. He found it far more exciting than his school book which was filled with religious stories and fairytales.

He read through the four badly printed pages. The paper called for a revolt. It implored workers and sailors and soldiers to rise up. His heart burned with excitement as he read the words. He wished that he had written them.

By now it was bright. The stockings and boots which he had placed beside the billy stove were warm. He pulled them on. His feet felt comfortable. Then he slipped on his long coat which the local tailor had made from a military overcoat and put on his felt cap. Vasily had no intention of going to school. It was too cold and he disliked his teacher, who was a drunkard and beat him when he was in a bad mood.

He left the cabin and entered the lane way. It ran between badly built cabins which had been constructed quickly from fresh timbers. They had warped during the years and all the buildings now looked grey and tatty.

Vasily trudged through the mud and snow. When he reached the banks of the Neva, the river was covered with a hard crust of ice. Skaters glided along the surface, calling out in delight. He gazed at them for a moment and wished that he knew how to skate. The grace and beauty of the skaters caught his imagination.

He lifted his head and scanned the cityscape with its great palaces and church domes and the high steeple of Saint Peter and Paul's fortress. Despite his hunger, he took delight in the beauty of the city and the balance of the buildings.

He walked across the great bridge which led from the Exchange to the Hermitage, the splendid city palace of the Tsar. A light snow was falling which was carried downriver by the wind. The cold wind cut at his bones and Vasily hurried forward.

Suddenly a troop of Cossacks came into view. They rode proudly down the centre of the bridge. They were a frightening presence with their heavy swords jangling by their sides, their horse tackle bright and gleaming. Vasily had heard stories of their efficient cruelty.

As he passed across the square in front of the Hermitage, he recalled the story of the massacre of 1905 which had taken place there. Young and old had been slaughtered by the troops of the Tsar and he had been dubbed "Nicholas the Bloody" as a result of the massacre.

Vasily passed beneath the vast memorial arch which led to the Nevsky Prospect. Very few from the factory district ventured into this part of the city. They had no reason to come. He could smell the scent of fine bread and pastries.

A limousine pulled up in front of the baker's shop and a lady, who could possibly have been royalty, left the car followed by a maid. Vasily stared intently through the window. The lady seemed dominant and bossy. The shop assistants dashed about the shop and brought her pastries and bread. She made her selections with an imperious gesture of her finger. Her maid stood by while the pastries and bread were wrapped up.

Vasily felt hungry. He looked up and down the street – there were no soldiers in sight. He also noted that he could slip down a side street and reach safety if necessary. A friend of his who had been a thief had warned him once: "Never get trapped. There must always be a way out. Or better yet, two ways out!"

Vasily looked about him. He waited and watched. Inside the shop the lady was still giving orders. He followed her movements. She instructed her maid to carry the bread and pastries to the limousine.

Now the maid was on the steps. Suddenly Vasily charged forward, and, sweeping the box neatly out of her hands, he disappeared down the side street before they were aware of what had happened.

"Thief!" someone called out.

"Thief! Thief!" others caught up the refrain. Vasily looked about. A group of people were in pursuit. His heart was beating. Vasily ran down a lane and then into a courtyard. There was no escape.

"Quickly!" an old lady said. "In here."

He dashed into a small room, which smelt of boiled cabbage and grease, and took refuge behind a curtain.

"What are you looking for?" the old lady said to the pursuers when they arrived in the great courtyard.

"A thief. He came this way."

"No thief entered this building. You are mistaken. I am always watching. I would have noticed."

There were some further discussions with the old woman. Then the crowd melted away.

"Well, son, what have you stolen?"

There was no reason to hide anything from the old woman. She had a wizened face and a shrewd eye.

"Bread and cakes."

"Then let us eat them. These are bad times. I am hungry. My name is Madame Versky."

"I am glad to meet you, Madame Versky. You have saved my skin."

For a small woman she had a large appetite. They sat in the dingy room and ate the pastries. She kept some of the bread and the rest Vasily stuffed in his coat.

He was about to leave when she asked him, "Can you read and write?"

"Yes, I am very competent. I have been well taught."

"Then I think I know somebody who might have work for you. It is dangerous, but I can see that you do not lack courage."

"Does it pay well?"

"You will receive some food. Food is gold. You want to stay alive in this dreadful weather?"

"Yes, of course."

"Then take this offer. Remember, it is dangerous. The secret police are always on the watch."

He was surprised at the vigour of the woman and the sharpness of her mind. Here was a woman of education and standing.

"I understand."

"Good. Now, let me give you your first orders."

She opened an old battered chest filled with clothes

and pushed them aside. Beneath them lay some newly printed papers.

She drew out twenty copies and handed them to Vasily.

"You know where the barracks of the Volinsky regiment are? Go and deliver them to a man called Gleb Semenov. He is one of our associates. Keep them hidden under your coat. He will distribute them among the regiment."

"If I am caught, what will I do?"

"I don't know. They may be lenient. You may end up in the fortress of Saint Peter and Paul's. Remember, these papers may keep other young men from going to the Front to be slaughtered like cattle. My son was killed. Bring this bottle of vodka with you. It will serve as a bribe. The soldiers are easily bribed. It is the first thing you must learn in this game."

She took a bottle from her cupboard and handed it to him. "Everyone is open to corruption in this city. Always carry a bribe. Off you go now and when you return I will have some soup for you."

He ventured out into the street. He would help the cause. He was not certain of the cause but he would help it.

Vasily walked back to the Nevsky Prospect. The great thoroughfare had resumed its business. He mustered up his courage and passed the pastry shop; nobody noted his presence. Slowly Vasily made his way through the city to the barracks, passing along all the great boulevards of the city. Everywhere he witnessed the effects of war on the population.

Young men wrapped in rotting rags, their bodies scarred and mutilated, begged at street corners. The city seemed choked with such casualties.

Old women wearing coats and head scarves and carrying bags were standing in long rows outside the bakeries.

Vasily kept reminding himself that the Tsar was to blame for all this. He had seen photographs of the Tsar and his family. They seemed pleasant people, but he had heard evil stories concerning the family. While others starved, they ate the finest foods from golden plates using silver knives and forks.

He arrived at the side entrance to the barracks. As the old woman said, it was guarded by a large soldier with a moustache and beard.

Vasily approached the grim gate. The soldier looked at him with bloodshot eyes. It was obvious to Vasily that he was half drunk.

"What do you want? You are trespassing! I could shoot you, you know; life is of little value in Saint Petersburg." He cocked his rifle sullenly.

Vasily plunged his hand into his pocket and took out the bottle of vodka.

"I wish to see my uncle," the boy lied, presenting him with the bottle.

The sullen face of the soldier brightened.

"Ah, you have brought Gurzuv a present. Very well. But do not take long. I am off duty in an hour's time. And remember, life is cheap in Saint Petersburg. We have orders to shoot anyone who approaches the barracks."

Vasily slipped through the small door and found himself in a stable yard. It led to a main square surrounded by military buildings. He asked a soldier who was brushing down his horse where he would find Gleb Semenov.

"You would be advised to keep your distance from him," he warned. "He is a dangerous man."

He gave him directions. Vasily had never been inside a military barracks before. The parade ground where the inmates exercised was a vast empty space. He walked along the edge until he came to Block D. He entered and asked for his contact.

He was directed to the top floor and trudged up flight after flight until he came to the upper storey. There he knocked on the door and entered. It was a vast area. Small iron beds were ranged over the floor and there was a strong smell of stale sweat in the place. At the far end of the room about twenty men sat about a small stove. They looked at Vasily and one man drew his pistol.

"I have come to see Comrade Semenov," Vasily stated loudly.

He walked down along the narrow space between the beds and arrived at the stove.

"What have you got for me?" a soldier asked.

"These," he said producing the newspapers.

"Good. Can you read?"

"Yes."

"Well then, read them for the men."

Vasily looked at the faces of the soldiers. They were hardened by war and violence. He began to read the paper for them. The writing was simple and to the point. They understood the message: "Join the people and lay down your arms. All workers of the world unite."

They nodded their heads in agreement.

"He is a good writer. He knows what he writes about and speaks for us all. The government is in the pocket of the Tsar. We have no voice," one observed

"You talk like that and you will be shot for treason," Gleb Semenov said.

"Better to be shot for treason than to die of hunger or on the Western Front. If one must die, he should die in the comfort of his own home," the soldier replied garrulously.

They laughed at his point.

"If we turned against our officers, we could take over the barracks," Gleb Semenov suggested.

"Would the other blocks join us?" one of the company asked.

"They read the same papers. They have no wish to go to the Front," Gleb Semonov told him.

"And the barracks about the city?"

"There is unrest in many of them. I have been in contact with them all," Gleb told them. "When the first officer is shot, then all the commanders can be on the look out. It needs only one spark to blow up the whole rotten system."

Vasily listened wide-eyed to the conversation. He had never been so close to revolution in his life. He felt exhilarated.

Gleb looked at his watch.

"It is time for you to go. Soon Gurzuv will be coming off the watch. Tell Dimitri what you have heard and what you have seen."

"Who is Dimitri?"

"The old lady will explain everything to you."

With that mysterious statement Gleb led him to the door. Vasily made his way down the stairs and along the path he had taken through the stable yard.

"You met your uncle?" the large soldier asked.

"Yes," Vasily lied.

He made his way back through the city to the courtyard where the old woman was waiting for him.

"I met Gleb Semenov," Vasily said. "I gave him the papers. Who is Dimitri?" asked.

"You wish to meet him?" the old woman asked.

"Yes. I'm to tell him what I have seen."

"He publishes this paper. He is a revolutionary. The police are after him."

"I would like to meet him then. I have read his paper. I believe in his ideals."

"Tomorrow you will meet him. He needs a young man he can trust. Now, here is your pay."

She handed him a loaf of dark brown bread.

It was worth its weight in gold in Saint Petersburg. Vasily now had enough food to feed himself and his mother for two days. He drank a bowl of soup and talked to the old lady. She was a very interesting person and possessed a small library of books. She lent him one before he departed.

He did not make his way home immediately. There was always so much to see on the Nevsky Prospect, the most important street in Saint Petersburg. Despite the cold, he noted that a circus had arrived in the city. It made its way down the main street with an elephant at the end. Vasily wanted to see the huge elephant up closer. He had not seen one before. He walked beside it and looked at its rutted skin, its large tearful eyes. He knew that elephants came from Africa and wondered if the elephant felt the cold of Northern Russia beneath its grey skin.

Later, he made his way home along the canals. They were frozen over and skaters were skimming along beneath the bridges. Again he envied them their freedom. He arrived at the Cathedral of the Resurrection. His mind could never grasp the intricacy of the bulbous towers, the ornaments and the arches. And then there were the glowing mosaics with their great religious figures. Today the towers were capped with snow and the scene was perfect.

He passed beyond the cathedral and entered the Champ de Mars. He walked amongst the trees and enjoyed the great park with its tranquillity. Some day he promised himself, he would know the names of all the trees growing here.

It was late when he crossed the bridge and made for the industrial district of Vyborg. A cold wind was whipping the fine snow off the road. It blew against his face in tiny shards. At last he reached the factory district. He looked at the great stacks still belching smoke into the bellies of fiery furnaces continually stoked by black figures. Even at night time the men worked at the mouths of these furnaces, feeding them until dawn.

Vasily left the main road and made his way through the warren of cottages and houses. Finally he came to the row of shacks in which he lived with his mother. As he approached the house, he knew something was wrong. There was light in the windows and a huddle of people outside the door.

"Is it you, Vasily?" a neighbour asked.

"Yes, what's wrong?"

"It's your mother. Your mother . . . " was all the neighbour could say.

Vasily pushed through the crowds. His mother was lying on her small bed – dying.

"What happened?" Vasily asked, kneeling at her bedside.

"A beam from the factory roof came crashing down. It fell on her chest," a neighbour whispered in his ear.

His mother's breath was shallow and irregular. A small drop of blood trickled down the edge of her lips. She stared blankly at the wall.

When Vasily appeared, she held his hand.

"Do not talk, Mother. I can take care of myself. Look what I brought you . . . " Vasily took out the loaf of brown bread and placed it on her hand. She felt the weight of the precious object.

With a small gesture she suggested that it should be shared with the neighbours. Vasily took the bread and broke it into lumps and passed it amongst those present. Then he drew out the white bread which he had stolen and also divided it amongst the neighbours.

Vasily's mother died at dawn. Immediately the crowd began to pray. Later more practical concerns occupied their minds.

"She did not belong to a union. She is not insured," one man said. "If she were insured, then they would pay her burial expenses."

"We all should belong to a union; we have to work in terrible conditions. The beam in the roof has been rotten for years; it was an accident waiting to happen."

"Surely the owner will pay for her burial," Vasily said.

"No, your mother was of no importance to him. There are several others who will take her place."

Vasily had now to consider how to defray the expenses. They had no money. Early the next morning he went to a money lender, a small hunchback who lived in the district. He had married a young woman whose parents had owed him money.

"What do you want?" the hunchback asked suspiciously.

"Money, to bury my mother."

"Money costs money."

"I will pay you back."

"When?"

"Over the next year."

"I do not trust you. You are a bad bet. What would you use for collateral? You could run away. No, I cannot lend you money. Ask someone else."

Vasily left the money lender's shop with anger in his heart. More than ever he hated the evil system which left him without enough money to bury his mother. Vasily decided that he must meet Dimitri.

He told an old neighbour to sit by his mother's body. Then he hurried across the city. His heart was charged with primitive emotions: sorrow, hate, rage and now doubt.

Arriving at the courtyard he met the old lady.

"I must meet Dimitri," he said.

"Why? Why the urgency?"

"My mother has died. I am an only son and I do not have the money to bury her."

She studied him intently. "Very well. I will bring you to him."

They took a tram to the edge of the city. From there they passed down a lane beside the tram stop. Soon they were in a small industrial compound.

"They print books here," she said.

Madame Versky directed him to one of the buildings. She opened a door and they entered the printing works. It smelt of ink, paper and hot metal. It was a spacious, confused place with awkward printing machines. Madame Versky knocked at a door and they entered an untidy office. An old man sat at his desk. He possessed a patriarchal beard and had small glasses perched on the end of his nose. He was proof-reading a long column of newsprint. He lifted his eyes and looked from the old woman to Vasily.

"This is Vasily," Madame Versky said. "He is our latest recruit. He is very capable. He wishes to speak to you."

Vasily told the old man his story.

"I fight against these evil things. Everything must be changed. You wish to come and work with me – I will teach you to be a printer. Perhaps you could become a writer. The pen is as mighty as the sword! Do you read?"

"Yes."

"Then you must read Pushkin. He is the poet of Saint Petersburg." Dimitri handed Vasily a copy of his works. "It was printed in this workshop. I am proud of such work."

Vasily studied the slim volume with the tooled leather cover. There was gold lettering on the spine and a crest on the cover. The pages were crisp and fresh.

"And now here are some roubles. You give your mother a good burial and buy her a fine coffin. I would have gone to the funeral but I cannot walk as well as I did. My feet have gout."

He handed Vasily a roll of roubles bound in an elastic band.

"There is six months' wages. You pay me back over two years. Understood? And if you wish to have somewhere to sleep, you can sleep here at the works. I need someone who will watch over the place at night time. I need a keen eye and a sharp ear."

"I shall come and work for you as soon as my business is finished," Vasily said.

Vasily and the old woman left the shop and headed up the lane together. His heart no longer raged. He could not believe his good fortune.

"Who is Dimitri?" Vasily asked as they waited for the tram.

"Dimitri is a Jew. He does not suffer from gout; he lost his toes in the deep frosts of Siberia where he was a political prisoner. He has suffered for his beliefs. The secret police still keep a check on him."

"But he is an old man."

"He is a writer. Writers can be dangerous people. The gift of writing is the most precious of gifts. It is given to some and not to others."

"How does one know if he possesses this gift?"

"You will feel the urgency to write. The impulse will push you to express yourself on paper."

The conversation would have continued but the tram arrived and they rode into Saint Petersburg and they were separated.

When Vasily arrived home, the old neighbour was still sitting beside the corpse of his mother, keeping vigil.

"Had we any visitors?" Vasily asked.

"No. Everyone is working. They cannot take time off."

For the first time since his mother's death, he had time to weep. He sat near the head of her bed and looked at her beautiful face. Hunger had defined the cheekbones and sharpened her features.

She had been born in a village in the south, though she had only a vague memory of it. She said that it had been a sunny place and a great monastery stood on a hill at the centre of the town and a wide river passed through it. The monastery housed a sacred icon.

Vasily's mother had been orphaned and sent to Saint Petersburg at an early age. She often sang songs which she remembered from her childhood. Her life had been confined to the cottage and the factory. She had rarely walked down the Nevsky Prospect and had never bought herself new clothes or eaten fine food. All her life she had worked at a factory loom. Despite the hardship she endured, she had never lost her dignity and had never raised her voice in angry protest.

He wept silently for an hour as he recalled the simple events in her life. When the old lady left the cottage, Vasily locked the door and went in search of a coffin at the carpenter's shop. He walked amongst the coffins which stood by the wall and picked the best.

"It is expensive," the carpenter said.

"I can pay for it," he said, taking out his roll of roubles and peeling off the amount required.

"I will have Igor deliver it to the house," the carpenter said. Igor was a huge, strongly built man with one leg shorter than the other.

They placed the coffin on a handcart and pushed it through the muddy and rutted lanes to the house.

Vasily paid an old woman to wash his mother's body and prepare it for burial. When he returned with some food for the wake the body had been placed inside the coffin.

That night the neighbours came again to the house. Vasily, who had not slept for two days, fell asleep. When he awoke it was morning. Followed by a small retinue of people, they set out for the cemetery. The priest read some prayers over the grave before cold clay was shovelled over the coffin.

When the crowd dispersed Vasily stood alone in the snow-covered graveyard. The snow lay softly on the arms of the crosses and the tops of the tombstones. From the graveyard he could see the great domes of the cathedral of Saint Isaac's and the cathedral of Our Lady of Kazan floating above the city. He was alone in the world.

He made his way home through empty lanes. When he arrived at the cabin, he discovered that it had be burgled by somebody. They had taken the few objects of worth.

"I hate this place," Vasily hissed between clenched teeth, looking around at the miserable cabin.

He took the book which Dimitri had given him, placed his mother's photograph and a lock of her hair between the leaves and put it in his pocket. He gathered his clothes and placed them in a sack. He looked about for a moment. Then went outside, closed the door, and set fire to the cabin.

CHAPTER 3

Nicholas looked out from the window of his palace at the still landscape. His mind was filled with dark unpleasant thoughts. Only the company of his wife and children gave him pleasure. They often read to each other or played simple games. He wished instead that he could go south with his family, to the Crimea where they had been happy. Each day, despite the heavy snow and difficulty of the route, ministers and the generals made their way to Tsarskoe Selo in the hope that the Nicholas might have some miraculous answer to their problems. But the time for miracles was over.

The war had been a disaster. It was winter time and the troops were stuck in muddy trenches to the west and to the south. To the north, in Saint Petersburg, things were coming apart. The hard winter was taking its toll. The railway system was falling into chaos. Food was rationed and fuel was scarce. Everywhere people were beginning to talk of a revolution. They would assassinate the Tsar and place his wife in a convent. The Tsarina, many felt, had taken too great an interest in the affairs of state.

"She is German," they said. "She is not one of us. She does not know how the people think and of their love of Russia."

Even the Tsar's relatives felt that there must be a change in the government. But Nicholas made no firm move. He lacked energy and decisiveness. He could not make decisions. Instead, each day he left the palace and walked through the woods. There in the great woods his problems seemed to vanish. He felt close to nature. When the war was over, he would go to the Crimea. He would walk in the gardens and life would be simple once again.

He left the map room and walked down innumerable corridors before arriving at the main entrance to the palace. Everywhere were servants waiting to attend to his needs.

His daughter Anastasia saw him passing and ran along the corridor after him. She was a vivacious girl, full of wit and charm.

"Where are you going Papa?"

"I am going to walk to the hospital."

"Can I come with you?"

"Perhaps you should not come. It is not a place for you."

"But I have often been there before, Papa. I have helped mother with the bandages and I have played billiards with the soldiers."

"Very well, come along then."

A servant fetched Anastasia's long coat and fur cap.

"I am ready, Papa," she said, smiling up at her father.

She was a short, plump girl with startling blue eyes.

The doors were opened and they walked out on to the palace steps.

"I have made friends with some of the soldiers at the

hospital. I often play billiards with them. I wish I were a qualified nurse like Olga and Tatiana. Then I could work in the operating theatre."

Nicholas fought back tears beginning to well up in his eyes. His daughters had been well brought up. Their education had been strict and they had slept in simple beds. They had never been spoiled and their hearts were not selfish. Russia could justly be proud of them. He wished that some of the ladies in Saint Petersburg had been so caring.

"Perhaps your presence may give heart to the soldiers."

"They are courageous men, Papa. They have fought bravely for Russia."

"I trust the soldiers. It is the members of the government I fear."

"Then why not sack them? You have the power."

"That is a difficult task. It is all very complicated." He spoke in a tired voice.

Anastasia did not pursue the topic. She kicked up the snow in front of her. Then she skipped forward.

More than his empire Nicholas loved his wife and his family. If only he could remain with them instead of wage the bloody war which seemed to have got out of control. He could not tell his wife how desperate things were at the Front. He wished that he could abdicate and spend his life quietly with his family.

Each day some general or other brought wretched news to him.

"Shall we go to the Livadia Palace when the summer comes?" Anastasia asked.

"Yes. We will go to the Crimea. We were always happy in the Crimea."

The red-bricked hospital came into view. It had

been set up in their estate by his daughters. As they approached the hospital, two ambulances arrived from the station. Nicholas and Anastasia made their way slowly through the snow and stopped in front of the hospital.

"I think we should wait until they have been carried inside," Nicholas said. He did not want his daughter to see the devastation of war.

"You need not fear, Father. I have been with the wounded before as they were carried into the operating theatre."

Nicholas realised that his daughters had been tested by the war. They were more familiar with its horrors than most young women in Russia. Suddenly he realised that his youngest daughter was no longer a child.

Nicholas and Anastasia approached the back of an ambulance. The doors were drawn open and inside they could see the wounded lying on stretchers. Two nurses came down the steps and assisted the ambulance drivers to carry the wounded into the hospital.

Suddenly a whisper passed amongst the wounded men lying in the ambulance.

"It is Tsar Nicholas," they said. "He has come to visit us."

A weak cheer went up from the men. The Tsar went forward and shook the men's hands as they were taken from the ambulance.

They followed them into the small hospital. It was a modern, well-aired place. At first Nicholas did not recognise his two daughters, Olga and Tatiana, who were dressed as nurses.

"Have you come to help us, Papa?" Olga asked.

"I am afraid I would be of no use."

"I have to go to the operating theatre. One of the soldiers has to have his arm amputated," Olga told him.

In the meantime Anastasia had slipped ahead into the billiard room. Nicholas followed her. When he entered, some of the men tried to rise from their seats.

He told them to remain seated. Anastasia introduced them to her father. She knew most of them by name.

"I believe that you have taught this young lady how to play cards?" he said.

"Yes, your majesty. Now she can beat us at our own games."

Nicholas sat with them and asked about their regiments and on what front they had fought. He was interested in every detail. His eyes seemed to brighten when he spoke to the soldiers.

"It is time for us to return," he told his daughter later.

They left the neat hospital and walked along the path towards the Alexander Palace.

"I have always loved this palace," he told Anastasia. "Saint Catherine the Great's Palace is larger and more magnificent, but I have always felt at home here."

As they approached the main entrance, they noticed a car making its way along the avenue.

"Who can this be?" Nicholas asked. "Another official from the government? I wish winter were over."

They walked up the steps of the palace and the servant took their coats.

"I shall see you this evening," he told Anastasia before making his way to the great map room where he studied the progress of the Russian armies ranged along a thousand mile line. He often met officials here.

Anastasia decided to listen in on the conversation.

She knew this wasn't a proper thing to do, but could not resist the temptation. She knew a secret compartment which her mother had had specially built so that she could listen in upon the meetings in the map room. Politics were not secret, she decided.

She made her way up the wooden steps and into the curtained gallery above the map room. From there she could look down on the great billiard table covered with maps. Her father stood by the fire, smoking a cigarette. His expression was tense.

"A Mister Rodzianko to see you, your majesty," announced one of the servants.

"Very well. I will see him."

A gentleman was shown into the map room. He was a fat individual with heavy jowls. He carried a briefcase and bowed stiffly from the waist.

Anastasia could feel the tension in the air. She had heard of Rodzianko. He was chairman of the parliament at Saint Petersburg.

"I am sorry to seek this meeting, your majesty, but it was necessary that I speak with you."

"Our meetings are never pleasant, Rodzianko," Nicholas replied.

"That is because I do not flatter you. I tell you things as they are. Others will conceal the truth. They think that the troubles will disappear. But I can assure you, your majesty, that things grow worse by the hour in Saint Petersburg."

"What do you want, Rodzianko?"

"I want a new voice for the people. You are surrounded by corrupt men. They give you bad advice."

"And you think that I should give power to the parliament?" Nicholas's voice rose incredulously.

"Yes. We are the elected representatives."

"And would you wrest the throne from me?"

"I hold a middle course. There are others who would have you jailed."

Anastasia gasped. Jail her father? She had seen him pace the corridors at night worrying about the fortunes of the war.

"You are a brave man to utter such words. I could have you arraigned for treason."

"That would be only too easy. Have you no idea what is going on at this moment in the city? In the barracks they talk of revolution. All they need is a single spark. The war has turned them sour. Each day there are more casualties. Everyone in the city has been touched by the war."

Heated exchanges between the two men lasted for well over an hour.

"And the Empress should not meddle in politics," Rodzianko declared. "It is not her business. She issues orders without your knowledge. She should be sent away. You believe that all is well and feel well defended with Cossacks about the estate, but there are very few others who will defend you now."

"You have courage, Rodzianko. You have said things to me which no one else would dare utter."

"Why do you think we are at present in this desperate situation?" the minister concluded.

"The parliament is against me. You seek power. How do I know that you don't wish to take advantage of this desperate situation?"

"You mistake my intentions, your majesty. I have come here in good faith. I think only of the future of the crown and of Russia."

"I should disband the parliament," the Tsar said.

"You would be making a great mistake. Soon any

rogue will be able to take over the country. I believe that this may be the last report I will make to you."

"Why?"

"Because you have not listened. You wish to dissolve the parliament. If you do, chaos will descend on Russia. A revolution will break out and you will reap the negative results of what you have sown."

"Well. God grant . . . " the Tsar began.

"God will grant you nothing; you and your government have ruined everything. There will be a revolution. That is all I have to say. Good day, your majesty."

Rodzianko bowed, took his briefcase from the table and left the room.

Anastasia was stunned at the conversation. What did it all mean?

Saint Petersburg was a beautiful city. It would not rise against her father. He had been appointed by God; surely no harm could befall him.

She watched him as he slumped on the armchair beside the fire. Suddenly he looked very old.

That night they had a very pleasant and intimate meal. The conversation was spirited and her father seemed happy again. Anastasia looked for traces of worry on his face, but they seemed to have disappeared.

Nicholas enjoyed his remaining days at Tsarskoe Selo. He went for long walks with the girls through the woods. At night they sat about the fire and he told them stories.

Alexei was in good health. As he sat with them, it did not seem apparent that he had been so ill, that once he had been at the point of death. Some day he would make an excellent tsar.

Yet, despite the pleasant times, visitors continued to arrive at the palace. One evening Nicholas said to his family, "I am tired of these endless visitors. I will return to the battle front."

"Will you take Alexei with you? You know how he loves to be with you and his presence heartens the troops," Alexandra said.

"I will be away for only a short time. I wish to escape from all these visitors."

He had made his decision. There was a tearful gathering in the great hall as Nicholas prepared to depart.

They watched him climb into the automobile and wave goodbye. They watched the automobile disappear down the avenue. There was a winter mist floating above the ground and it seemed to disappear into its magical centre. Nicholas could not know that he would soon return to Tsarskoe Selo, but not as Emperor. Dark forces were at work which could not be controlled and the world of the empire was coming to an end.

CHAPTER 4

Vasily stirred in his bunk. For a moment he thought he was in the fetid cabin in the industrial district. Then he noticed the white light of the snow reflected on the ceiling. He remembered that he was in the printing works and recognised the dry odour of ink and metal. Turning over in his bunk, he looked down at the machines for typesetting; the great drums which printed the paper; the large white bales of paper standing like marble columns in the corner of the room, the pots of metal which could be melted and moulded into letters.

He had been a week in the workshop. Each night he took a ladder and climbed to a wide open loft above the office where he had set out his mattress. It was warm in the recess. Above all he enjoyed the great space of the printing shop. The air was filled with rich, mysterious scents which were becoming familiar to him. He stirred in his warm bed before throwing aside the blankets and clambering down the small stairs to wash himself. Then, having dressed, he began to arrange the small blocks of timber over a heap of paper in the billy stove. He lit the paper and soon the room was warm.

Vasily made himself a warm breakfast of gruel which he ate with relish. As he ate he considered his good fortune. He looked at the machines, sleeping like great animals. Soon they would waken, soon there would be a buzz of activity and the workshop would whir with noise.

Having eaten his breakfast, he tidied away his dishes, then set the pots of metal to melt on the stove.

His fortunes had changed in a single week and his mind was filled with enthusiasm for the new work. Never before had he met a group of people so dedicated to their work. Vasily felt he was part of this group. They believed in a revolution and hoped that the whole rotten imperial system would collapse some day.

They were interested in every scrap of information from the capital. A phone brought in news from all over the city. Each morning Dimitri and his sub-editor Ivan sat about a table and considered the situation in Saint Petersburg. It seemed that trouble was brewing in the barracks and in the factories. The time was ripe for a revolution.

The printers began to arrive, shaking the snow from their great coats and complaining about the weather.

Pavlov, who was a typesetter, arrived with a piece of interesting news.

"The Tsar has left for the Front. I heard it from one of the Cossack soldiers at Tsarskoe Selo."

"He has left Saint Petersburg in the hands of a corrupt government. He should have taken action. He has made a grave mistake," Edvard the printer shook his head in dismay.

"He made a serious mistake the first day he ever took charge of the army," Dimitri told them.

"Kerensky is calling for the assassination of the Tsar. And his is a moderate voice," Pavlov added.

"Nicholas should have remained in Saint Petersburg. His presence alone would have restrained the crowd," Edvard said.

"No. It has gone too far. Too many have died and suffered. The peasants have gone to war and there is no one to till the land. Women cry out for bread. All it needs is a spark and the whole rotten system will come crumbling down," Dimitri told them.

"What shall we write today, Dimitri?" Pavlov asked. Dimitri put a sheet of paper in his battered typewriter.

"Let me see now," he said, scratching his white beard. He closed his eyes and searched for an idea. Vasily watched in awe. He never tired of watching Dimitri at work.

"Let us call on the army to join the people," he said at last.

There was a murmur of consent from the others and Dimitri began to clatter away at the typewriter. Words seemed to flow from his chubby fingers.

After about forty-five minutes he took the page from the drum and handed it to Pavlov.

"I have used large letters. This is not the time for small print and unnecessary details."

Now Pavlov sat in front of the typesetting machine and set out the front page. The pewter-coloured letters fell into place. In the meantime Dimitri and Ivan worked on other material which had already been prepared the day previously. The print drums were ready and inked. Edvard began to print the first edition of the paper.

By now Vasily was familiar with the operation. As the wet pages rolled off the press, he took them and folded them. Then he rolled them up into bundles and pushed them into his haversack.

"Never get too confident. Remember the eyes of the secret police are everywhere. They would quickly haul you off to jail," Dimitri warned.

"I know. I can sense danger."

Dimitri gave him a handful of kopecks for his fare. Vasily stuffed a sandwich in his pocket and left the print works. He had never felt more secure or happy in his life. He trudged through the snow towards the tram stop. Soon he was on his way to the centre of Saint Petersburg.

Snow lay heavily on the rooftops and on the streets. Soldiers on crutches begged at every street corner. The people looked hungry and cheerless.

Vasily quickly delivered the papers to the various depots. Then he returned to the Nevsky Prospect. He loved the architecture of this street. It enchanted his eyes and he never failed to find something new to look at. Now that he was reading the works of Pushkin, he was eager to visit all the places associated with his name. He could already recite large sections of his magnificent poetry.

Vasily was standing before the Bronze Horseman in Senate Square when he saw the mass of workers from the Vyborg district crossing the Neva bridge. They were carrying flags and banners. He rushed along the riverbank and watched them push across the bridge in great waves. They were chiefly women and they called out, "Give us bread. Give us something to eat!"

It was the cry of starving people.

Vasily had never seen such a massive demonstration. It was like a great sea beating against the walls of the city. He quickly followed them down the Nevsky Prospect. They crammed the street and pushed the police aside; traffic was brought to a halt.

All the time they chanted, "Give us bread. Give us bread."

He looked at the faces of the women. They were drawn and hungry and they reminded him of his mother. They had come to the end of their patience.

He watched the demonstration for two hours. They continued their chant. A group broke into a bakery and emerged carrying loaves of bread. At any moment he expected the Cossack regiments to descend upon the Prospect on horseback and use their whips on the backs of the people as they often had done before. But they did not appear.

He waited for the crowd to disperse. They melted from the centre of the city and passed across the bridges to their districts. He took the tram and hurried to the printing works. He told the story to the men.

"And were they not fired upon?" Dimitri asked.

"No."

"Then the soldiers may be coming over to the workers' side. Tomorrow I want you to go to the Winter Palace Square. There may be another march. We need an observer on the spot."

"But I have never written anything important in my life. What will I say?"

"Observe everything, particularly the small details. Write down what you see. And stay with Madame Versky. She will have accommodation for you."

That night Vasily did not sleep very well. Life was becoming intense and exciting. He was living at the hard centre of history. He wondered if he could catch the times in words.

Next morning he set off early for the city. Dawn was breaking and a mist lay about the trees and above the buildings. The city was almost deserted. He took his position at the Winter Palace close to the bridge.

Soon the great city came to life. Automobiles and carriages began to move across the bridge. A squadron of soldiers marched across the square and under the Admiralty arch to some barracks or other. An old woman in amorphous clothes, her back bent, trudged through the snow. Vasily stamped on the ground to keep warm. He began to form sentences in his mind. He tried to describe the scene. He recalled Pushkin's description of the city in his poem "The Bronze Horseman". Yes, he would use some of his fine lines and expanded them.

He did not have to wait very long in the snow. Soon a mass of workers began to move across the bridge. Mostly women, they were angrier than on the previous day. He noted students in their midst calling out familiar slogans. Some called for the death of the Tsar and his German wife.

He sensed the anger amongst them and he followed them down the Nevsky Prospect. Every time they passed a baker's shop they looted it. They smashed windows, pushed open the doors and emerged with baskets of bread.

Together they cried out. "Our children will not starve!"

At midday the Cossacks appeared. For about ten minutes people feared that there would be a bloodbath. The Cossacks always suppressed demonstrations in a brutal manner. They were feared by everybody, but Vasily noticed that they did not carry their whips. They called out familiarly to the crowd.

"Don't worry. We won't shoot!"

It was at that moment that Vasily knew that a profound change had taken place in Saint Petersburg. The Cossacks, who had been the protectors of the Tsar and who had suppressed rebellions in the past, were now on the side of the people. The little newspaper and all the other papers had had their effect. The world had changed. The world had changed on Friday 9 March 1917 and Vasily had been there as a witness.

When he reached Madame Versky's house he realised that he had not eaten his bread. He took it from his pocket and broke it in two halves. "You eat," he told the old woman. "Share my bread."

The old woman accepted the food. "You are a generous youth," she said. "Soon this dreadful war will be over. The great wheat fields will be planted again and we will not starve. Then there will be bread for us all."

He sat beside her near the small fire and she spoke to him of her youth in Saint Petersburg. She had been there on Bloody Sunday when the troops had opened fire on the people.

"It was a peaceful demonstration. The people came with their crosses and icons and religious banners. They held portraits of the Tsar above the procession. And as they moved along they sang "God Save the Tsar". The soldiers opened fire and on that day my belief in the Tsar died. That is why I am a revolutionary."

It was late when Vasily went to bed.

The next morning, Saturday, he awoke early. He felt that there would be more trouble in the city. He was correct.

When he emerged from the flat and moved on to

the main road, he noted how quiet things were. The trams had stopped running and the trains remained in the stations. The city was paralysed. Suddenly great crowds charged with anger surged through the streets like waves. They carried red banners and cried out: "Down with the German woman. Down with the war!" Vasily had not realised that Alexandra was so hated by the people.

This was no longer a sea of women crying for bread; these women were crying out for blood. There was a sense of anger. They were harangued by mob orators who shook their clenched fists vigorously in the air. Nothing was certain and no military action had been taken.

The Cossacks and other regiments remained in the barracks.

Night fell. Vasily was not to know that the governor of Saint Petersburg had received orders from the Tsar to quell the riots. As a last resort, the soldiers would use rifles and machine guns. Sunday would test the city.

Vasily made his way to the heart of the city in the morning. If there was trouble it would begin here and Dimitri had told him to document every incident. Already he had filled several pages of a notebook with details.

All over the city were huge posters banning meetings. Crowds gathered before them disregarding the notices, planning . . . on the Nevsky Prospect.

"Will the soldiers obey orders?" Vasily asked a wounded veteran who moved about quickly on a crutch.

"Not on their own people. They will come over to our side."

He spent the day with the crowd, then towards

evening it happened. A regiment of soldiers moved down the Prospect. They were grim-faced and carried guns. He would never forget what he witnessed next.

At a signal they knelt down and fired into the crowd. People screamed. Beside him a woman was shot. Vasily looked at her helplessly. People milled about him as he tried to protect her. There was another volley of shots. More people fell beside him.

He lay amidst the dying and the dead, hoping that they would give him cover.

There was silence. He looked up over a dead man. The soldiers were moving away from the Prospect. He was stiff with fear and could barely move.

He looked at the woman. She was dead.

Vasily moved away from the carnage. There was blood on his coat and on his shoes. All around him people moaned in anguish. Saint Petersburg was ready to erupt.

Vasily later discovered that not all the soldiers had turned their guns on the people. Some regiments had shot their commanders. Others had mutinied.

That night an uneasy peace settled on the city. In the barracks the soldiers argued. They decided that they would not fire on the people again.

It happened suddenly and early on Monday morning. The Volinsky regiment rebelled. They were the most respected soldiers in the city. They killed one of the captains and the rest fled the barracks. Then they marched out of the barracks with a band playing and joined the revolution. Revolt spread like wildfire. All the great regiments joined the rebellion.

Vasily was on the Alexander Bridge when the revolutionaries and the army came together. They built the first barricades and soon after they began to burn many of the great buildings of the city: the law courts, the headquarters of the secret service and many other government buildings.

All day long Vasily observed the revolution in progress. No one ruled and everyone ruled. Members of the cabinet resigned.

Vasily wondered what would happen next. He knew that the parliament was meeting in the beautiful Tauride Palace. Suddenly he heard a brass band. It came around a corner to a firm march. Behind it marched workers and soldiers carrying their red banners and singing the "La Marseillaise." A young sailor called to Vasily. "Come and join the parade. This is the first day of freedom!"

He was a bright-eyed young man who was clearly enjoying the first day of the revolution.

Vasily joined him. He felt suddenly that he was part of the new Russia. The mass of marching men about him, the music, the sound of the singing made him feel he belonged to the common people. He knew that they were all moving towards a great change.

"Where are we going?"

"The Tauride Palace."

"And what will happen there?"

"I don't know, but something is bound to happen."

He looked forward, took up the marching step and began to sing loudly.

"Things will be different from now on," the young man said later when they had finished singing. "This is a day I have long waited for. The city is ours. The old government has fallen. It was rotten. Now parliament will rule,"

All about him agreed.

The band turned left and they marched in through the gates of the Tauride Palace. It was a long yellow palace with a shallow dome. Vasily was struck by its beauty. He had often observed it from a distance. Now he was marching up to the great façade with its Greek columns.

They walked straight into the main hall.

It was a gorgeous palace with chandeliers and large delicate windows. The place was swarming with soldiers and students. Here and there were a few old men with large watery eyes. They had recently been released from prison.

Vasily entered the magnificent hall which housed the parliament. He looked at the confusion about him. Nobody seemed to know what was happening.

"Kerensky must solve our problems," somebody shouted.

He had heard of Kerensky, who was an important man. He arrived at the palace and tried to establish order. Vasily found himself at the very centre of power. Men of no great stature were suddenly running the country. It took Kerensky all day to solve the problems of parliament.

That night there were two assemblies trying to rule Russia from the palace. The workers and the soldiers set up their own council.

More confusion followed. The old government members came to the Tauride Palace for protection. Yesterday they had been the most powerful men in Russia; today they were prisoners.

The soldiers called out for their blood. They would have bayoneted them in the corridors, but Kerensky intervened and they were saved for the moment.

That night Vasily, weary from the day's events, made his way home to the printing works. Saint Petersburg was in the hands of the revolutionaries. He had much to report to Dimitri.

As he looked out the window of the tram at the confused city, he wondered what had happened to the Tsar and his family.

CHAPTER 5

The magnificent imperial train sped through the night. As it passed through the blackness of the Russian landscape, the Tsar felt broken-hearted. He thought of his family at Tsarskoe Selo and wished that he had remained with them and that the war was over.

The train was truly fit for a tsar. It had been constructed in the workshops of the Alexandrovsky Mechanical Works in 1896. Images of the double eagle were emblazoned on the sides of the carriages. The Royal bedroom was vast, the tables made from Karelian birch, while the corridors were lined with grey silk wallpaper. The Emperor's room was faced in American walnut and the furniture upholstered in dark green leather. Ornate lights hung from the curved ceiling. No expense had been spared on the luxurious fittings.

The train, which had carried his family all over the empire, was a lonely place. Nicholas missed his son Alexei. He had travelled with him many times to the Front dressed in his military uniform. A great bond had developed between them. He had slept near him at the head quarters in a simple camp bed.

Nicholas sent a telegram to Alexandra from the train.

51

"Feel again firm, but very lonely. Thank you and baby for the telegrams. Am terribly sad. Kiss you all tenderly."

Then he received news that Alexei had caught the measles. Soon the rest of the family were stricken by the same illness. It was a source of anguish to him. He would note later that the end of his empire began with the illness.

No sooner had he reached headquarters than his wife was sending him news from Saint Petersburg that 80,000 workers had gone on strike. There was no bread to be had in the city.

Each day new telegrams arrived; Nicholas felt lonely and frightened. He didn't know what to do.

His chest pained him and he began to perspire. He wondered if he should abandon his position at the Front and return to the capital city. His presence there might restore order. He had no one to talk to and he could trust no one. He was beset with enemies and problems. Despite his anxiety, Nicholas was unaware of how bad things were in the capital. Such details were kept from him. All about him on the Front were the casualties of war. Each day soldiers died. Each day soldiers were maimed and each day hostility grew stronger.

He walked alone along the mud paths in the forest. His face was creased by worry and his mind was tired. A pain throbbed at the back of his head. The weight of the empire was too heavy a burden for him to carry. Soon a decision began to form in his mind. He would abdicate. He would hand the throne over to someone else. His wife and his family were more important to him than power, pomp and splendour.

News continued to flood in. Order was breaking

down. No one could halt the tide. Nicholas ordered the train to take him back to Tsarskoe Selo. He wished to be with his wife and children.

Nicholas could not know then that there was trouble at his beloved Tsarskoe Selo. On 14 March the garrison of 40,000 men rebelled and rebellion had reached the gates of the peaceful palace. The Empress could no longer ignore the gravity of the situation.

The phone rang. Fat Rodzianko, who had spoken so forcefully with the Tsar a fortnight before, explained the situation in the city.

"What shall we do?" a marshal asked.

"Tell Alexandra to flee with her children."

"They are sick with the measles. They cannot be moved."

"Better sick than dead," was the reply.

The Marshal put down the phone. His mind was in turmoil. He rushed to the Empress and told her of the conversation.

"I am not going anywhere," she replied. "I will stay with my sick children. Let the revolutionaries do what they will. Have the Cossacks turned on us as well?"

"No. They still guard the palace."

"Then our lives are spared for the moment."

Alexandra received further news from the capital. The mob had thrown open the prisons and there were red flags everywhere.

Daylight came. The white snows about the palace turned to silver. The woods were peaceful. The revolution seemed a hundred miles away. Now and then the sound of fire echoed through the silver birch. Then there was silence; it was a silence filled with fear.

About the palace grounds the mounted Cossacks stood guard.

At nine o'clock the inspection of the troops began. The Cossack regiments had held firm, but many of the other regiments had deserted.

The Empress emerged from the palace later that night, a coat draped across her shoulders, to inspect the troops. A lantern was carried before her as she passed before the regiments. Her face displayed a quiet courage.

When the inspection was finished, she called the officers and said to them. "Gentlemen, please, there is no need to shoot. No matter what happens. I do not want blood spilled because of us."

Then she retired to her rooms.

"Something terrible is happening," Olga told her sister, Tatiana. "I have listened to the conversation of the servants. Some of them have already fled the palace. They say that Saint Petersburg is in the hands of revolutionaries."

"What will happen to us? What will happen to Father?" Tatiana asked.

"I do not know."

"Then we must be brave."

"I fear that something dreadful is going to happen," Olga cried.

"We must bear everything with dignity."

"No. They will know soon enough."

That night they slept intermittently. The morning was to bring further trouble.

Alexandra's favourite regiment, under the command of Grand Duke Kirill, had left the barracks. They were marching to Saint Petersburg to join the revolutionaries.

Now only two infantry battalions remained. The palace could be stormed. Alexandra began to fear for her children. She tried to contact her husband but only received the reply: "Place of Residence unknown."

Enemies were setting a ring about her. Tragedy was closing in about them. She could sense it in the air.

Night fell. Alexandra passed through the rooms and visited her children. They were anxious about the situation.

"What will happen to us?" Maria asked.

"Nothing will happen. Soon your father will return and all will be well again."

Alexandra needed all her courage to hold back her tears. Later she walked to the door of the palace and looked down the avenue. She expected some danger to emerge from the darkness.

Suddenly the headlights of a car lit up the pathway. She wondered if this was the end as the car came to a halt at the foot of the steps.

A general stepped out of the car and was ushered into the palace. He told Alexandra that her husband's train had been surrounded at a small station a hundred miles from the city. All over Saint Petersburg the servants were fleeing the palaces. The aristocrats stood alone. They were helpless. A bloodbath was expected at any moment.

"What shall I do? Where can we go?" Alexandra asked. He did not answer. "Is it that bad?" she asked.

"Yes. I fear the worst. The situation has deteriorated rapidly. I felt I must warn you."

He said good night and left the palace. She was alone, surrounded by enemies, and her children were ill.

She returned to her rooms and prayed before her icons.

Nicholas had set off from the Front in the Imperial train. He wanted to be with his family. Reports continued to flood in. Everywhere the revolution was spreading. The people were calling for his abdication.

The train passed through the darkness. Outside, snow lay over the great flat plains of Russia. He was not certain if the train would be able to get through.

"What is the news?" he asked one of his commanders.

"The rebels are taking control of the stations. Lyuban and Tosno have been taken. They are manned by soldiers with machine guns."

Nicholas studied a map.

"Let us go through Pskov," he ordered.

The soldier left the carriage and carried the news to the drivers. The train moved forward, coming to a halt at Pskov.

It was eight o'clock. The station was almost empty. No guards of honour were there to present arms.

The Emperor's face was grim. A pain pounded his chest. His personal guard had abandoned him and the capital lay in the hands of the revolutionaries. He was alone.

Nicholas decided to phone Rodzianko, who had spoken so openly and directly to him ten days before. He wired the Duma headquarters.

He would offer old Rodzianko a new parliament and a new prime minister.

The messenger returned from the telegraph office ashen-faced. He handed Nicholas a telegram.

"His majesty is apparently unable to realise what is happening in the capital. A terrible revolution has broken out. Hatred for the Empress has reached a fever pitch. To prevent bloodshed, I have been forced to arrest all the ministers. Do not send any more troops. I am hanging on by a thread myself. Power is slipping from my hands. The measures you propose are too late. The time for them is gone. There is no return."

Nicholas read the telegram over and over. Here he was isolated at a railway station while his fate was being decided many miles away in the capital.

Events were now beginning to move rapidly. Telegrams arrived from all his generals in the battle fields. They wished him to resign. If only Alexandra were with him; she would give him solid advice.

It was three o'clock. He went to the window of the train and looked out. Then he turned around quickly and said to those present, "I have decided to give up the throne."

It was a final and fateful decision.

News of the decision reached Saint Petersburg. The night the governing body decided to send Guchkov and Shulgin to travel to Pskov and witness the abdication.

The day passed. Those remaining with Nicholas at the station waited expectantly for something to happen and lights come on in the Imperial train. Outside it grew cold and then it began to freeze. Nicholas left the train and walked up and down the dark platform in order to stretch his legs. His face was tightly drawn and tired. He wished that the whole business was over. As Nicholas was walking on the platform, the locomotive from Saint Petersburg arrived at the station of Pskov. It drew a single car.

Two men dressed against the cold Russian winter emerged from the carriage. They moved towards the Imperial train carrying briefcases.

"This way, gentlemen," a member of the staff directed. They entered the green parlour car. Shulgin, who was one of them and would later recall and set down each detail of what occurred, noted that the walls were covered with green silk. He observed that Nicholas was wearing a grey Circassian coat; his elbow was propped against the wall. There were bags under his eyes and the Tsar looks ill and exhausted.

Guchkov and Shulgin talked to the Tsar for some time.

Nicholas listened impassively. "Give me the manifesto of abdication and I will read it in my study," he said, taking the fatal document. He retired to study it. Later he returned and signed it. Once he had signed the document, he felt the heavy burden of responsibility fall from his shoulders. He was now citizen Romanov.

"I have signed away my empire," he declared. "Now, what will follow?"

The meeting was over. A coat of varnish was placed over Nicholas's signature.

Shulgin and his companion left for Saint Petersburg.

Nicholas had one final gesture to make. He wished to say goodbye to his armies.

As the train moved on towards Mogilev, the Tsar wrote in his diary: "For the sake of Russia, and to keep the armies in the field, I decided to take this step. All around me I see treason, cowardice and deceit."

His mind brightened when he met his generals. He felt free in the freezing conditions of the Front. They noted how haggard he looked and how hollow his eyes appeared. He glanced at them and accepted their salute.

For five days Nicholas remained with his generals.

One day a train arrived at the station. A corporal hurried to Nicholas.

"Your mother has arrived in her private train," he told him.

Nicholas rushed to meet his mother at the station. He climbed on board her train and she met him with tears in her eyes. "What have you done, Nicki?" she said. "Could you not have held out a little longer?"

"The burden was too heavy to bear. Now I feel as if a heavy weight has fallen from my shoulders. The generals and the cities have turned against me. Michael, my brother, will be Emperor."

"And your own son? You have taken the throne from him."

"That too was necessary. He is ill. We will go to the Livadia Palace in the Crimea. There we can have a pleasant life together. I think only of my family."

"And what of your mother? What of all the others?"

"They helped to bring this about. My very family plotted against me. I am now citizen Romanov."

"You have humiliated me. Your father would not have taken the easy way out. He would have fought against these revolutionaries. His armies would have marched on Saint Petersburg."

"It is over, Mother," Nicholas said with finality.

"It is not over. What will become of us?"

"You will be taken care of."

"I doubt it greatly. We should have never entered the war. You were all fools. You, the Kaizer, Franz Josep. You could have patched up your quarrels."

His mother had become an old woman. Even the regal bearing, for which she was famous, had disappeared.

After the outburst she began to weep. Great sobs

shook her body. She wiped away the tears with an embroidered handkerchief. She looked weak and vulnerable.

Nicholas lit a cigarette and looked out the window but he did not see the landscape. His eyes looked inward and his mind was almost at peace.

His mother, Marie Fedorovna, remained at the station for three days.

During this time Saint Petersburg turned further against the Royal family and there was a very real fear that they might be massacred at Tsarskoe Selo. The provisional government decided to arrest Nicholas and return him to the Alexander Palace.

He was with his mother when they arrived from Saint Petersburg to take him prisoner.

"I must leave you now, Mother," he told her. "They tell me I have to return to Tsarskoe Selo."

"Tell you! Tell you! Once they would have fallen on their knees at your approach."

She began to weep. He put his arms about her and held her. Then they said goodbye.

He left meekly and climbed aboard the Imperial train and set out for Tsarskoe Selo. He was now a common prisoner. He would never see his mother again.

CHAPTER 6

"Vasily! Vasily," Dimitri called excitedly.

"Yes," the boy replied from his bunk.

"Nicholas has abdicated. He is no longer Emperor!"

"Then we are free?" Vasily asked, knuckling the night's sleep out of his eyes.

"We are never free. But we have a new government. We may yet rule ourselves."

"And Nicholas, what will happen to him?"

"I don't know. I want you to find out. These are exciting times!"

Dimitri began to light the fires in the grates. Soon the print works smelt of burning newsprint.

Vasily climbed down from the loft and made his way through the printing presses to the barrel of water which stood outside the door. He broke the icy crust with an axe and washed himself. The cold water sharpened his senses.

He looked about him. Snow had fallen during the night and everything had a soft edge. Only Dimitri's footprints franked the snow. Vasily loved such mornings when the light was pure and sharp.

He recited some of Pushkin's poetry and danced on the snow and moved his arms briskly to keep warm.

In the distance, Vasily watched Pavlov make his way up the small avenue, his heavy Russian hat over his ears, his breath forming a large plume in the air.

"You have heard?" he called.

"Yes, Dimitri told me. The Tsar has abdicated. Is it not wonderful news?"

"Wonderful beyond words. A new dawn has broken."

By now Pavlov had reached the printing works. They went inside and Dimitri prepared a simple meal for them: bread, eggs and milk which he had purchased from an old woman the night before.

"What news do you bring from Tsarskoe Selo?" Dimitri asked.

"It is confused. Everywhere there is gossip."

"Have the Royal family fled?"

"There is nowhere they can flee to. The workers have taken over the railroads and they will not let them move."

"So they are prisoners?" Vasily asked.

"They are isolated in their own town," Pavlov told them.

"And the Tsar? Where is he?"

"He will join them later."

The other workers soon arrived. They too had stories to tell. Before they began work, Dimitri opened a bottle of vodka. He lined up the tin mugs from which they drank and poured each of the workers a drink.

They lifted the mugs and saluted.

"To the revolution," Dimitri called.

"To the revolution," they answered.

Then they set about their work. The whole printing works was in a happy mood. They no longer feared the secret police. Now they could publish their paper without being hassled.

*

"Shall I go to Saint Petersburg and find out what is happening?" Vasily asked Dimitri.

"No. That is a dead story. The people are no longer interested. I wish you to go to Tsarskoe Selo. Try and discover what is happening there. Write down everything you see and hear and bring it to me. And remember the advice I gave you. Look for the telling detail. Write simple Russian that simple Russians can understand."

"Very well. But how do I get to Tsarskoe Selo during these confused times?"

"You are a bright lad. You will find a way. And wear a red band about your arm. Here is some money."

Dimitri took some roubles from his purse and handed it to him.

Vasily thanked him and left the printing works.

His life had changed in the past few months. He no longer felt insignificant. He had tasted the power of words. He had read some of his own work in the paper. Dimitri was a good teacher. With a sweep of a pencil he would put a thick mark through paragraphs and sentences.

"Simplify. Simplify," he would say as his eyes passed over a page.

Before he left, Dimitri gave him some food wrapped in an old newspaper which he placed in the pocket of his coat.

Vasily left the printing works and joined the main road south towards Tsarskoe Selo.

As he trudged through the snow, Vasily pondered how the revolution had made no apparent difference. Life seemed to continue as usual. An old woman with a humped back carried a bundle of faggots home for her fire. Children threw snowballs at a blind man and ran away laughing. A gentleman in a fine fur coat drove past in his carriage.

Vasily noted a carter approach; a heavy man with a square beard and a scar on his face. He drove a small determined horse and a tarpaulin covered the truck.

"Are you going toward Tsarskoe Selo?" Vasily asked.

"Yes, comrade. I carry food to our troops. They stand guard about Bloody Nicholas's palace. Are you one of us?"

"I was in Petersburg when the revolution took place. I was there when the troops slaughtered the people."

"Then you are one of us." The cartman moved aside, making room for Vasily on the cart.

"Push your back into the tarpaulin; it will keep you warm. And take some bread. It has been freshly baked, but keep it covered. It is as precious as gold. People would kill for it."

Vasily ate some of the bread. It was crusty on the outside and soft inside.

The carter sang a moving old Russian song which was sad. Meanwhile the sturdy little horse made its way through the snow, moving south at a slow pace.

Vasily looked about. The light played on the landscape and turned it into a luminous white. Here and there a golden church dome wore a cap of snow. The birch barks were burnished with silver. The heart of the woods and copses seemed mysterious. Vasily had never been in the presence of such beauty before. His life had until now been confined to the district of smoke and furnaces and the stench of filth. Here he could almost smell the snow.

He and the carter talked as they drove. The carter, whose name was Maxim, had been to the wars.

"And what have I to show for it but a wooden leg

and a cheap medal? But we went to war with good intentions: wanted to die for Mother Russia. It was terrible – I could tell you stories which would make your hair stand on end."

A black line appeared on the horizon. As it grew larger, Vasily noted five horsemen advancing. They looked menacing as they approached. The horses kicked up the thick snow about them and their tackle sparkled in the sun.

"Keep your head down. Pretend you are a peasant. They could be the enemy. Tell them nothing. I will say that you are a deaf mute."

Now they could hear the jingle of the horse tackle.

"They are Cossacks. Dangerous fellows," Maxim whispered out of the corner of his mouth.

Vasily watched them approach. They surrounded the cart.

"Are you a foe or friend?" the Cossack leader asked.

"I am a simple peasant setting about my business."

The leader noted the red band on Vasily's arm.

"Then you are one of us."

"Yes, I am one of you and so is my friend," Vasily told him. "We carry food to the soldiers."

"Good. Follow us. There are marauding bands in the vicinity. Some vow that they will kill the Tsar. Others will kill friend or foe for the few kopecks in their pockets."

"What is the news of the Tsar?" Vasily asked.

"You mean citizen Romanov," the Cossacks corrected.

"Yes. Citizen Romanov," Vasily said.

"He is expected to return to the Alexandra Palace this evening. That is why we keep an eye out for strangers."

"And his wife and children?"

"They are prisoners. Soon the people will decide

what should be their fate. You ask many questions for one so young."

"I report news for a paper. My editor sent me to Tsarskoe Selo."

The Cossacks were hungry. They lifted the tarpaulin and helped themselves to the bread. Then they led the cart forward.

"The Cossacks were once loyal troops. Now they have changed sides. They are with the people. I have seen them charge at innocent people and cut them to pieces," the carter whispered.

After a while Tsarskoe Selo began to emerge in the distance. First it was an outline of trees, then buildings. It stood above the plain. The roads had been cleared of snow and they could advance more rapidly.

Vasily's eyes were filled with wonder. Everywhere along the road stood the great houses of the nobility. The wonderful washes of green and blues and yellows on their walls stood out against the trees and the snow.

"What has happened the servants?" Vasily asked.

"They have fled. Once they heard that the Tsar had abdicated, they took to their heels, carrying with them what they could. Two days ago these houses were humming with life. Now they are great empty mansions."

Vasily studied everything carefully. The street lamps, the shops, the railway station. Everywhere troops seemed to be on the move. They were disorderly in manner and carelessly uniformed.

One group approached the cart.

"What have you got there, comrade?" a rough soldier asked one of the Cossacks.

"Bread for the army."

"We are the army. Feed us now that we are all

comrades," he growled, urging the men to attack the cart.

The leader of the Cossacks took out his revolver and pointed it at him.

"One move and you will not live to see another dawn," he told him.

He slunk away like a weasel.

"Who needs comrades of that ilk?" the Cossack commander asked.

They finally reached the store. The bread was taken from the cart and placed behind locked doors.

"You have done well," the Cossack said to the driver. "Tomorrow you can return with another delivery."

"Perhaps there will be no bread tomorrow," Maxim told him. He spoke in a fatalistic voice.

Vasily sat with the Cossacks who had belonged to the crack regiments. He listened as they discussed their future.

"Order is breaking down. You have seen it with the soldiers. They answer to no one. I do not trust them. They have no respect, not even for women. I was there when twenty of them arrived from Saint Petersburg and visited the palace. They treated the palace as if it were a stable and abused the Royal family. They need a new leader."

Vasily left the Cossacks' barracks and began to explore Tsarskoe Selo. Whenever a soldier challenged him, he pointed to the red band about his arm. He could not believe that such order and beauty had existed in the world. Tsarskoe Selo was more than a village; it was a town. Every mansion, palace and shop was beautiful to look at. Great trees stood in parks and along avenues. The gardens were laid out in squares and circles and triangles. The hedges were trimmed and statues stood at intervals along the boulevards or in the centre of open spaces.

Vasily felt that he possessed the whole of Tsarskoe Selo. He passed into the grounds of the Palace of Catherine the Great and made his way along the central path, with formal gardens running on each side. The snow lent the gardens a bright, magical quality. Vasily looked about in awe.

On an incline stood the enchanted building of the Catherine Palace. The façade seemed to stretch forever to the left and the right. Rows and rows of white pilasters and pillars were set against the blue walls. Gold leaf gleamed on ornament and cornice. The great windows, high and spacious.

He moved up the steps on to the foundation on which the great palace had been constructed.

Vasily's heart was filled with magic and wonder.

Suddenly a shot rang out. He dived on to the snow and heard the sound of army boots rushing through the snow.

A rifle barrel was placed at his temple.

"Rise slowly," the voice said.

He got on to his feet. Two soldiers stood facing him.

"He's just a lad," one of them said.

"He could be the cursed Prince," his companion said.

"Who are you, lad? Speak up."

"I am Vasily from Saint Petersburg. I work for a local newspaper. I have come to report on the Tsar and what has happened at Tsarskoe Selo."

He took out his notebook and pencil and showed it to them. Both were illiterate.

"Write our names for us," they said.

They told him their names and he wrote them down. They studied them from every side and smiled.

"You are a bright young lad. You will go far," the leader told him.

Vasily produced a small bottle of vodka.

"I have brought a present for you. It is cold guarding such a palace. You need warmth within."

They took the bottle eagerly and passed it between them.

"Can I enter the palace?" he asked.

They became suspicious.

"Are you a thief? The village is filled with thieves bent on stealing what they can lay their hands upon."

"No, I am not thief. I give you my word. I would just like to see the palace. I have never seen anything like it."

"You go with him, Nikolai. Guard him well," the soldier said.

Nickolai walked with him to the great door, took a key and unlocked it. It swung open slowly.

"I will smoke my pipe while you visit the place. I have no interest in such things. I wish to get back to my village and prepare the ground for sowing."

He took out a short pipe and lit it. Then, sitting down on a great ornamental chair and crossing his legs, he began to smoke.

For the next hour Vasily passed through the most beautiful rooms he had ever seen in his life. They were breath taking. The great windows were flooded with light. He stopped in the centre of the Throne room and gazed about him at the great mirrors in their gilded mouldings. As he walked across the parquet flooring, the sound of his steps re-echoed sadly from the walls.

The amber room took his breath away. Every object

was made from the precious material. Vasily touched them. They possessed a soft velvety quality.

Vasily grew dizzy. There was too much to see in so short a time. The light was beginning to fade and he knew that the waiting soldier might be getting restless and irritable.

He hastened through the corridors and down the white baroque state staircase to where the soldier was still sitting smoking his pipe.

"I'm sorry to have kept you waiting," he said.

"Not at all. It is warm here. I was freezing in the sentry box. You were lucky I was cold; I aimed to kill but my fingers were numb."

With that he knocked the ashes of his pipe on to the marble floor, put the pipe in his pocket and they walked out the door together.

It was evening and the lights were coming on all over Tsarskoe Selo.

As he passed through the village, Vasily entered a small shop to buy tobacco for the soldiers. He could use it as a bribe to gain entrance to various buildings. The shopkeeper was a suspicious man.

"I do not have tobacco. I have nothing. I have been looted," he said.

"I have money," Vasily said, producing a roll of notes.

"Are you armed?"

"No. Search me if you wish."

"I believe you."

He went into a back room and returned with some tobacco.

"It is exclusive," the shopkeeper said. "I stocked it specially for the nobility."

"The nobility no longer exists. I was in Saint

Petersburg and I saw it all happen. They have fled from their palaces. Many have been captured and some were shot."

"Terrible. Terrible. What will happen the Tsar?"

"I do not know. I suppose he will be tried."

"And the beautiful Princesses?"

"I do not know."

"They are simple gentle girls. They often called to my shop. They turned some of the palaces into hospitals, you know. Two of them are trained nurses. One of the servants told me they sleep in iron beds"

"I did not know that. You mean they washed and cared for the wounded."

"Yes. And spent nights by their bedsides. Their ladies in waiting would not do the same."

"Where are they now?"

"In the palace. They are ill with the measles and the young Prince is not well. He has the bleeding ailment. If he falls, he bleeds within. Great black marks form on his body. It is very painful. The monk, Rasputin, could heal him, but he is dead."

The information fascinated Vasily. In one sense it was information he did not wish to hear. He had built up a picture of the Royal family. Now the shopkeeper was placing doubts in his mind.

In Saint Petersburg it was easy to hate them. In the Tsar's village of Tsarskoe Selo the Royal family seemed human and vulnerable.

"And the Tsarina. She is very brave. Nicholas is away and the soldiers have turned against them. I hear all the gossip from the palace "

"Where do they live?"

"Six hundred yards from here in the Alexandra Palace. It is up the road."

Vasily left the shop and walked up the broad avenue until he found himself in front of a large iron gate. This was the entrance to the Alexander Palace.

Guards stood about the gates. They carried loaded guns and close at hand behind a wall of sandbags stood some soldiers with machine guns set. They had lit a brazier and were standing about it.

"What has happened?" Vasily asked a soldier.

The soldier hit him on the side of the face with a rough hand and Vasily fell to the ground.

"Do not mind him," a black-toothed soldier said, helping Vasily to his feet. "He was drinking all day and has a bad head."

Vasily took some tobacco from his pocket and offered it to the soldier.

"Smells good," he said, opening the packet.

"I purchased it in the village. It was meant for the nobility."

"I will enjoy it the more," he said, filling his pipe.

"What is happening here?" Vasily asked.

"Nobody knows. Today the new guards took over. They are raw and dangerous. No one can control them. I fear the worst. They could organise a firing party and execute the Royal family. They are a bad lot."

"What is happening at the palace?"

"Today the Royal family were made prisoners. Their loyal guards and many of their servants have left them. Those who remain are prisoners."

"Have you seen them?"

"I was nursed by them. When I returned from the Front with a broken leg, the Tsarina insisted that it should not be cut off. Both she and the two eldest girls washed out the wound and drew away the poison. I may have a limp but I still have my leg. Now they are alone. They are the loneliest people in Russia."

"I wonder what is happening in the Palace?" Vasily asked, looking up the avenue. In the distance he could see lights in the windows.

Although he did not know it, the Empress was standing at the window looking down at the roofs of Tsarskoe Selo. Her heart and mind were heavy.

Tomorrow her husband would return. He had been stripped of his titles and his empire.

She longed to meet him. Their love had never wavered through all the years of marriage and during the last terrible year of the war.

She had taken the girls aside and told them the dreadful news. They had wept when they heard what had happened, but resolved to be courageous.

Alexei heard the news from his school teacher, an Englishman called Sydney Gibbes. He could not grasp why his father would no longer be tsar.

"But if there isn't a tsar, who's going to govern Russia?"

His tutor tried to explain that a new provisional government had been formed in Saint Petersburg, but Alexei could not understand.

At four o'clock the day they became prisoners, the doors of the palace were locked on them.

They were left the use of one wing; the rest of the palace was off-bounds for them. Elsewhere in the building their guards were drinking. They had visited the wine cellars and carried bottles of wine to their quarters. They broke the necks and drank directly from the bottles. Sometimes they poured the precious wine out on to the floor, calling for vodka.

They were little better than rabble.

The great palace had become a prison. The Empress walked throughout the corridors of their wing. The corridors were empty except for a guard who tramped up and down in heavy boots. Most of the servants had fled. Alexandra was anxious about many things. Her children were ill with measles and earaches. They could not move until they had recovered. And she worried about her son. He bruised so easily. She had seen him in agony, his body wracked with pain after he'd bumped against some object.

And how would her daughters hold up under the ordeal? They had been reared in a simple fashion and had had nothing to do with the problems which now devastated Russia.

"It is a nightmare," she said to her lady-in-waiting, Baroness Buxhoeveden, who had remained with her.

In a short few days their world had come tumbling down about them.

The Empress stood at the window. It was night of deep frost. The parkland sparkled in the moonlight.

For twenty years she had enjoyed great happiness in Tsarskoe Selo. It had been a pleasant place. Somewhere in the distance there was the rattle of gunfire, then silence. Alexandra returned to the mauve room. Her sleep was troubled by nightmares.

CHAPTER 7

Somewhere a trumpet sounded. Vasily began to stir in the hayloft belonging to the Cossack regiment. The night previously he had climbed up to the loft and wrapped old horse blankets about him against the cold. The hay smelt dry. For a moment he thought that he was in the printing works. He blinked in the grey light which poured through the windows. Standing up, he shook the hay from the blankets and from his hair.

Then he made his way down the wooden steps and past the horses. Outside he found a barrel of water and, having washed himself, studied his situation.

Very few soldiers were stirring in the village of Tsarskoe Selo. He decided to visit the railway station. Tying his red band about his arm, he made his way along the road. The surface was as hard as iron from the frost. He picked his steps carefully and noted the black smoke curling up from the chimney at the railway house. He approached cautiously. Everywhere was empty. Even the guards had left their posts. He stood on the platform.

"You!" a voice called out. "Who gave you permission to enter this area? It is out of bounds you know."

Vasily turned his head quickly in the direction of the voice. The stationmaster came down the platform towards him, dressed in his uniform and looking quite troubled.

"I have come from the barracks," Vasily said. "I have come to study the area."

"You are very young to be a soldier."

"I am a stable boy. My master sent me to observe things. I write down what I see. They say that today Nicholas arrives."

"That is so. They say that he is no longer Tsar. I cannot believe that such a thing could happen."

"Times will get better," Vasily said.

"Times never get better. You come with me and I will give you some warm milk and eggs."

They passed along the platform until they arrived at the stationmaster's house. It was a tidy place with official pictures of the Tsar and his family on the wall.

"I know the Royal family well. They have often passed through this private station. I have frequently spoken with the four sisters; angels they are. Have you read these rabid newspapers? Do not believe them. All lies. They spread scandal. The Romanov daughters are charming girls. I have seen Olga and Tatiana take the Royal train to Saint Petersburg for a ball at the Winter Palace when the roads were snowed in. They looked like something from a Pushkin fairy tale."

Vasily and the stationmaster were sitting and drinking milk when the sound of a soldier's footsteps on the platform interrupted them. A harsh voice called out and then there was a loud knock on the door.

The stationmaster opened the door and a coarse-tongued officer entered. He looked at the wall and cried out. "We no longer have a Tsar. The people now rule!" With that he went to the wall and tore down all the pictures of the Tsar and his family.

"They are commoners now. They will eat what we eat; they will travel the way we travel and they will work as we work."

The stationmaster was angry. He stood up and faced the soldier.

"The Tsar was a good man," he said.

The soldier hit him in the chest with the butt of a rifle. He fell on the ground. Vasily helped him to his feet.

The soldier looked at Vasily.

"Who are you?" he asked.

"I write for the newspapers," Vasily answered proudly.

"And what do you write?"

"I write what I see. I have been to Saint Petersburg and was there when the soldiers opened fire on the common people. I write about it in the papers."

"Who taught you to write?"

"A monk."

"Soon we will hang all the monks. We will turn the churches into stables. The people will rule."

The soldier possessed a brutal and stupid mind. Vasily would not argue with him.

"We have come to guard the station. Bloody Nicholas arrives at eleven. He is to be taken prisoner."

The soldier left the room and Vasily turned to the stationmaster. He was pale.

"Observe our new masters," the stationmaster said. "We will always have masters. Wait here with me and you will see the Tsar. There is nothing more beautiful than the Royal carriage. It is a mansion on wheels. I have sat in the great armchairs used by Nicholas and

Alexandra. I once felt proud of my position here. Now I am the servant of ignorant pigs."

The station began to become alive. People still turned up for work and went about their business.

Vasily watched time pass slowly on the clock. He took out his book of Pushkin's work and began to read from it. No sooner had he begun than some cars arrived.

"I recognise the cars," the stationmaster said. "They are from the palace garage, though I don't recognise the drivers. The Tsar must be due to arrive."

Vasily looked at the clock. It was a quarter to eleven. A phone rang. There was immediate activity on the platform. Soldiers checked their guns. Some looked menacingly down the line, others blew warmth into their hands or stamped their boots. Some smoked cigarettes.

At eleven o'clock the Imperial train arrived at the station, the Royal crest emblazoned on the front. There was a great hissing of steam and squealing of brakes as it drew to a halt. The carriages were painted in a mid-blue and the Imperial carriage was decorated with golden eagles.

The stationmaster had described the interior and exterior of the carriages so minutely that Vasily could identify each one; particularly that of the Tsar which contained two studies and a bedroom. The corridor was lined with grey silk wallpaper.

The Imperial carriage was directly opposite the window. Vasily looked expectantly at the door. The door was opened by a soldier and then the Tsar appeared.

Vasily was disappointed. Some peculiar image in his mind had made him believe that he would appear in splendid uniform with a crown on his head. Instead he was dressed in a soldier's great coat and a Caucasian fur cap. He was a man of slight build who seemed unsure of himself and looked anxiously about him. His skin was yellow and taut across his temples. For a moment he stood alone, then suddenly he was surrounded by a group of men.

An officer came forward and they handed Nicholas over to him. He was now a prisoner.

The whole procedure had taken very little time. The Tsar moved forward with quiet dignity. He entered a waiting automobile with two others and was whisked away to the Alexander Palace.

Vasily was about to follow when he saw the doors of the Imperial train open and people who had served the Tsar rush from the carriages, some carrying valuable objects they had stolen.

"Rats leaving a sinking ship," Vasily said to himself.

He watched them disappear across the tracks. They looked like scavengers.

Vasily began to feel pity for the Tsar – what would happen to him and his family? He had spent two days in the Tsar's village and the hardness he had once felt towards the Royal family seemed to have softened. He had come close to the very centre of empire and was beginning to have doubts about Nicholas. Vasily had seen the man. He looked ill, tired and frail.

Vasily rushed from the station just as a military truck was starting off for the palace. He rushed after it and some soldiers hauled him into the back.

"Are you one of us?" they asked.

"I wear the red band."

The truck moved slowly along icy roads. When they reached the entrance to the palace, they jumped from the back of the truck.

There was confusion at the gates. They had been locked by the sentry.

"Who goes there?" one soldier asked stupidly after he had opened the gate and come forward to the lorry.

"Nicholas Romanov," one of the passengers said.

"Are you certain it is citizen Romanov?"

"Yes."

"Then let him pass."

The gates swung open. The car and the lorryload of troops moved forward. Vasily was with them.

At the entrance to the palace they poured from the lorry. They surrounded the Tsar. The soldiers on duty moved towards him. They showed no respect: some were smoking pipes, while others wore their caps. Some spat in front of him.

Nicholas saluted them as he had been trained and they looked at him with boorish curiosity.

He walked up the steps with dignity and entered the palace – now his prison.

Those who had gathered about the door to stare at the prisoner lingered in groups before dispersing.

The spectacle was over.

"What will happen now?" Vasily asked one of the guards.

"We wait for our instructions. If we have to execute citizen Romanov, we will. He is an enemy of the people." There was no feeling in his voice.

Vasily decided to explore the grounds of the palace. He passed along the avenues which the Tsar and his children had often enjoyed. It was a pleasant place. He reached the children's pond with its delightful island in the centre. It was a magical place of bare willow trees, their branches arched and icicled. They looked like great chandeliers flashing in the sunlight.

The magic of the place moved Vasily. He had read the poems of Pushkin and he knew that he had lived close to the palace for many years in a dacha.

Vasily began to recite some of these poems as he passed through the enchanted grounds.

As he was returning along the central path towards the Alexander Palace, a guard suddenly appeared. Like the rest, he was rough-looking with a heavy moustache and a torn fur cap on his head.

"Have you permission to be here?" he asked loudly.

"No."

"Then I can shoot you on sight."

He cocked his rifle and aimed it at Vasily. For a moment the boy thought that he might actually fire. Times were dangerous and little regard was shown for human life.

Vasily stared at the soldier, who possessed Mongolian features. His eyes were hard and without mercy.

The soldier lowered his rifle. "Why waste a precious bullet on a lad? I will keep it for the Tsar. Come forward until I see you."

Vasily trudged up to him through the snow.

"Do you smoke?" Vasily asked.

"I smoke but I cannot afford tobacco. They do not pay soldiers."

"Then I have a present for you," Vasily said, taking a pouch of tobacco from his pocket.

The soldier's eyes gleamed with pleasure. He drew his pipe from his military coat and filled it with tobacco.

"This is good tobacco. Where did you get it?"

"I purchased it in the village."

"Have you any more?"

"No. That is all," Vasily lied. He was always conscious that he could be robbed by one of the soldiers.

"Soon we shall all smoke such tobacco. You come with me and I will show you to the gate. This is no place for a boy – it is dangerous."

They walked towards the palace. Suddenly they saw the Tsar, dressed like an ordinary soldier, marching down the steps and coming towards them.

The soldier sprang into action. Placing himself before Nicholas, he pushed the Tsar back with the butt of his rifle.

"You are not at liberty to walk here. I have my orders."

Vasily looked at Nicholas and felt great pity for him. Here was the mightiest monarch on earth being pushed about by a thug. Suddenly other soldiers emerged from the woods. They pushed and shoved Nicholas. Then they shouted at him as if he were a subaltern.

"Back! We don't permit you to walk here."

The Emperor did not say a word. He looked evenly at each one. Then, turned and walked back to the palace. Vasily watched until he entered the building.

"We taught that fellow a lesson," one of them said.

"Who does he think he is?" another asked.

"We should have shot him when we had the chance. That would have put an end to him."

Vasily looked up at the palace window. He noticed a woman looking down on the group. Then she drew away, letting the curtain fall.

Vasily was about to make his way back to the village and find some food when three armoured cars arrived from Saint Petersburg. Several soldiers surrounded the car and cocked their guns.

"Who goes there?" a sentry asked. "What do you want?"

"Nicholas. We wish to bring him back to the fortress of Saint Peter and Paul. He is a criminal."

"Have you a warrant for his arrest?"

"This is our warrant," they said, pointing their guns at him.

"I cannot argue with guns," he said.

They were about to drive through the gates when an officer appeared with one of the household guards who had remained.

"You cannot take Nicholas. His children are ill. Have you no compassion?"

"Then we will see Nicholas," they insisted.

"Very well. I will make the appropriate arrangements."

Vasily heard later that Nicholas had been required to march past them as they stared at him before they departed. This assured them that he was a prisoner at the palace.

Satisfied, they then left.

For Vasily it had been a most exhausting day.

He returned to the village towards nightfall and found an abandoned mansion. He slipped around to the back, broke a window and entered. He found a lamp and lit it. It was a luxurious place, filled with gilt mirrors and silk drapes. Vasily climbed the stairs and let himself into a library. He had never seen so many books before. He wished that he could read them all.

Instead, he sat at a desk and, taking out his notebook, began to write an account of the day. It had been a day full of events. Vasily wondered what the Tsar and his family were doing at that moment.

What would become of them?

The lights not had been quenched in the Imperial Palace.

Nicholas visited his daughters who were still ill and lay in simple beds.

"What will happen us, Father? We are sorry that we are ill. We are a burden to you."

"Not at all. You are more precious to me than the whole empire."

"Is it true that you will never rule again?" Tatiana asked.

"I'm afraid that is true. I abdicated my throne for the sake of Russia. Let us hope that the Duma can put things right."

The Duma was the name of the parliament in Saint Petersburg.

"They never will," Tatiana said. "It is impossible to govern Russia."

"What will happen us?" Olga asked.

"Perhaps we will go to the Livadia Palace and live by the sea. Or perhaps we may travel to England. The British Royal family are closely related to us. I spent time in England when I was young."

"I would prefer to go to the Crimea. We could go for walks in the mountains and develop the gardens. The sun is warm in the Crimea."

"We shall see. Now go to sleep, you need rest. Today has been a most stressful day. Tomorrow things will look much better. It is time to sleep."

Nicholas left the sick room and called to see Maria and Anastasia. They were excited to see their father and threw their arms about his neck. They did not discuss the future but spoke of pleasant things. Later he left them and returned to his study where he sat with Alexandra before the fire and together they spoke of many things.

At last Vasily had finished his notes for the day. He was weary. An exploration of the mansion brought him to one of the bedrooms and Vasily crawled between the covers of one of the most luxurious beds he had ever slept on and fell asleep.

In a forest some distance away the body of Rasputin burned. He had been a strange figure, with his long, untidy beard and his mesmeric eyes. He alone with his hypnotic power could relieve Alexei of the terrible pains which wracked his body. In the eyes of the Imperial family he was a *starets* or holy man. To others he was a demon who had brought destruction on Russia. His influence over Alexandra had been immense. At one time he had almost controlled the destiny of Russia. That was why Prince Yussoupov and his friends had decided to poison Rasputin in the cellar of his palace. But he would not succumb to the cyanide they had put in his drink, so Prince Yussoupov had shot him. Even that failed. Rasputin crawled out of the cellar and made his way across the snow-filled courtyard. They shot him several times and beat him senseless with a club. Then they wrapped him in a blue curtain and, having dug a hole in the Neva, pushed him through. Three days later his body was discovered and an autopsy showed that he had died by drowning. He was buried close to the palace at Tsarskoe Selo. The soldiers had taken the body from its tomb in the Imperial park and brought to the forest. There they flung it upon a pile of logs, poured petrol upon it and set it on fire.

It would burn all night. Rasputin had predicted that he would be burned in this manner.

He had also predicted the destruction of the Imperial family.

In the early morning the wind blew his ashes through the trees.

CHAPTER 8

Vasily took the train to Saint Petersburg. He had remained two days at Tsarskoe Selo but the Royal village had become quiet. Behind the iron railings of the Alexander Palace the Tsar and his family were prisoners.

He had spoken to the inhabitants of Tsarskoe Selo and he had built up a picture of each member of the Royal family. He even obtained photographs of the Imperial family and had examined each face carefully.

As the train trundled across the snowy plain, he reflected on his good fortune. He was free. Life was opening up for him. The former ruler of Russia was a prisoner. He wondered what was happening at Saint Petersburg. The whole world was collapsing and he was at the centre of the storm.

Opposite him sat a woman looked anxiously about her. Every time the door of the carriage opened she became nervous. She was well dressed and Vasily could tell from her skin that she had lived an indoor life. Her fine fingers clutched a leather bag.

The door of the carriage opened and an officer stuck his head into the compartment while some soldiers moved along the corridor. The officer looked sullenly from seat to seat.

"This is her," he said, his eyes resting on woman. "This is the thief. She has stolen from the people."

He wrenched the bag from her hand. It opened and golden forks and spoons tumbled to the floor. She did not cry out but stared rigidly ahead of her.

"Gather up these stolen goods," the officer ordered. He grabbed her by the hair and threw her on the floor.

She collected the forks and spoons.

"Come with me," the officer demanded.

She followed him down the passageway. Vasily watched closely. Between the carriages the officer raised his pistol and shot the woman in the back of the head. Then he pushed her out the door.

"She was an enemy of the people," he told the passengers. "And she tried to escape."

Vasily was horrified. Life in Russia had no value any more. He had been taught by his mother to value it. Before, people wept when someone died and there was a sense of sorrow. Now there was no sorrow. He felt a chill about his heart.

He looked out at the vast snow-filled landscape, dotted with black copses. It seemed to stretch to infinity. He took out his volume of Pushkin and began to read. He loved the simplicity of the lines and their noble strength.

Finally the train reached the station. The passengers poured out. He noted that the captain and his men were laughing together.

"Old Rezov will buy them. He will melt them down and sell them as bullion," he told them.

Vasily walked through the station. The revolution had not changed Saint Petersburg. There was slush on the streets and the hungry were still begging for food. Eventually, he found a tram which took him to the outskirts of the city. From there he walked to the print works. The smoke was rising from the chimney and there was a strong scent of burning birch wood. He pushed open the door and went inside.

"You're back!" Dimitri said, looking up from his typewriter. "What news?"

"What did you see?" Pavlov asked.

"Almost everything," said Vasily breathlessly. "I was at the train station when the Tsar arrived and I was at the palace when they insulted Nicholas. They butted him with their rifles. There is so much to tell – "

"Did you write it down?" Dimitri interrupted.

"Yes. I wrote it all down, in a fine library south of Tsarskoe Selo in a mansion which had been abandoned." Vasily handed Dimitri his notebook.

Dimitri scanned through the notes.

"They are good. They are very good. Are you sure that the Tsar's skin was yellow?"

"Yes. It was yellow and old like crumpled paper."

"And Rasputin's body – is this true? Was it burned?"

"Indeed. It was as he predicted."

"Have you been to the forest where they burned it?"

"No, but I talked to a soldier who was there."

"It is a good story. We will use it," Dimitri said.

"And the rest?"

"Keep your notes. Write them up. Perhaps some day you will write a book."

"Perhaps he should write one on Rasputin," Pavlov suggested.

"It would be a good idea," Dimitri said. "There are lots of people in Saint Petersburg who knew him intimately. It is an extraordinary story how an evil-smelling peasant could weasel his way into the Imperial family. He had a strange power. I saw him many times," Dimitri mused. "You were always drawn to his piercing blue eyes. He also had healing power and could cure Alexei's pains. Alexandra listened to his political advice. He whispered in her ear and helped rule the country. That is why they killed him, but he would not die. First they poisoned him, then they shot him. Finally he had to be wrapped in chains and thrown into the Neva."

"Tell me more," Vasily said.

"He was born in a village in Siberia. He was a thief and a drunkard. Then he became a pilgrim and wandered Russia. When he arrived in Saint Petersburg he was introduced to Alexandra. He was pious and abstemious at the Imperial Palace. In Saint Petersburg he was a drunkard and a glutton. There is much more which I could tell you but I must refrain. There is work to be done."

Dimitri's words made Vasily curious. Dimitri had Vasily's story set up by one of the printers. When Vasily saw his story on the front page of the paper, he felt that he had truly come of age. Most of his words were there. They had been edited, but it was his style, simple and sharp like Pushkin.

He was growing up fast. Life at the print works was never dull. Each day Vasily learned more about the printing trade. He learned how to set type and read it backwards. He placed the type in the drums, inked them and started the machines. He fed the white sheets of paper through the drums and watched as they emerged printed. The words seemed to come alive on the pages. Every evening, in his own time, he read the Russian classics. They filled his mind with wonder and helped to form his style.

There were days when Dimitri might call and send him scurrying to Saint Petersburg to cover some story or other. Above all, he was learning the politics of the city.

"The world will be changed at the Tauride Palace," Dimitri told him.

Vasily became familiar with the palace and those who stood guard about the doors. He frequently paid visits to this seat of government.

He was never certain who ruled the new Russia. In one wing was the new government. In another was the Soviet or council, representing the soldiers and the workers. Both offices issued orders.

Soon it became obvious that the power lay with the Soviets. They had the ear of the people. And something else was happening. The revolutionaries who had fled Russia were coming home. They came from all over the world. One rode two thousand miles out of exile across the Steppes of Russia. Others sailed from New York or travelled from France. All their lives they had lived for the moment when they would govern themselves and change the world. Now they flocked into Saint Petersburg.

Vasily noted that the city did not improve under the new government. Signs bearing the legend "By appointment to His majesty Tsar Nicholas" were torn down; statues were toppled and destroyed, together with doubled-headed eagles.

The city was losing its lustre. There were demonstrations everywhere. The factories had more or less closed down and there was little order in the streets.

One day Vasily was walking through the corridors of the great palace when he heard somebody say, "Lenin is returning from Switzerland. He has been in exile there for many years. He's a firebrand. Now things will be stirred up. He will be arriving at the Leningrad Station."

"Then we will be there when he arrives," his friend answered.

Vasily decided to investigate.

The train would arrive in darkness. As he made his way across the bridge, Vasily saw the street lights reflected in the waters. It was cold and he drew his coat up about his ears.

He entered the station some time before the arrival of Lenin. Already it was crowded. Red banners were flying and there was a feeling of intense excitement about the place. And then at 11:10 p.m. Lenin arrived with the all the other exiles. He was a small man, almost bald, with a goatee beard and glittering eyes. The band began to play "La Marseillaise". The crowd descended upon him. Sailors from the Baltic fleet carried him forward. He climbed on to an armoured car outside the station and addressed the crowds.

"Let the workers take power. Let us end the war. Peace! Bread! Land!" It was a simple message.

The crowd cheered. Afterwards Lenin was whisked away in the armoured car. The crowd remained a while before dispersing. It was after midnight when Vasily reached the printing works. He let himself in, climbed the ladder to his bunk, and considered the happenings of the day before drifting off to sleep.

At Tsarskoe Selo spring came. The snows melted. Soon the first flowers began to show and the palace settled down to its own ritual.

The guards now took their prisoners for granted. At the start they had insulted them; they had even jeered and whistled as they passed by, but the Tsar never lost his patience or his dignity.

The girls had recovered from their illness and their good spirits returned. Anastasia soon got to know the names of her guards. Her directness and humour won them over.

The sun grew warm and it seemed that the troubled world of Saint Petersburg had melted away with the snow. Life was pleasant. Nicholas, no longer burdened by the affairs of state, had time to read to his family.

Every day they expected to be escorted to England or transported to their palace in the Crimea where the girls could finish their education and the young Prince Alexei gain strength. His sisters doted upon him. He was always the centre of their attention.

In May Vasily made a trip to the village of Tsarskoe Selo. It was a quiet place. At the gates of the Alexander Palace he met two guards and, producing a bottle of vodka, offered it to them.

"You wish to see the Tsar and his family? Very well. Igor will take you to the palace."

Vasily followed Igor through the grounds. The trees were in leaf and the perfume from the flowers filled his nostrils with their sweet scent.

"And what are Nicholas and his family doing?" he asked.

"Planting a garden. Every day he works in the garden with his family. The girls fetch water. Already the seeds are beginning to grow."

As they rounded a corner, Vasily was amazed by what he saw. The former Empress was sitting in a wheelchair watching her husband and children weeding the garden. She had become ill with the burden of life and often had to be pushed from place to place.

Vasily was surprised at the beauty of the girls. No photograph he had seen did justice to them. The place was filled with their laughter.

The soldier pointed out the girls by name. Olga was the eldest. She had chestnut hair and a wide Russian face. Tatiana worked beside her. She had sparkling blue eyes.

"She gives the orders," the soldier said.

Anastasia skipped along the edge of the garden while Maria carried water to the plants.

Vasily watched the Royal family with fascination. As he followed Igor back to the great gates later, he remembered each girl in detail.

"What will happen to them?" he asked the soldier.

"Your guess is as good as mine. It is up to Karensky to make the decision. He is in charge for the moment in Saint Petersburg. If Lenin takes over, it could be a different matter. We might get orders to shoot them."

"Would you shoot them?"

"No. But there are brutes in Saint Petersburg who would take pleasure in the task. Things change quickly from day to day."

Vasily left the village. Clearly he would have to keep a close eye on events.

He returned to the printing works and explained what he had seen to Dimitri.

"Very interesting. They have become pawns in a great game," Dimitri observed.

"How do you mean?" asked Vasily.

"They are related to both the German Royal family and to the English Royal family. Perhaps the English Royal family will intervene and do a deal with the new government. There is a chance that they may be saved."

"Do enemy nations talk during wars?"

"Of course they do. Much goes on of which we are not aware. You are young. You can move almost unnoticed through the crowds. Learn to be a master of disguise. Follow the events at Tsarskoe Selo, and watch Lenin. I believe that he is dangerous. He has no heart."

Vasily often sat with them and listened to them talk. They had differing ideas on politics and religion. They were well read men who loved the printed word and the paper they published.

Some thought that Nicholas should be executed. "It would mark the end of an empire. While he remains there is a threat," Pavlov said.

"And the family? Should they be killed?" asked a printer.

"No, just Nicholas."

"You think that then we will have a new world where all men will be free and equal. It is a hollow dream. Russia needs a strong ruler or tyrants will take over."

The controversy never ended. When the print works were deserted at night time, Vasily lit his lamp beside the billy stove and read. It was during these months that he would read all the great Russian writers. These writers became familiar to him: Dostoevsky, Tolstoy, Pushkin, Chekhov, Alexander Herzen, Chernyshevsky. Hour after hour he pored eagerly over the books. Sometimes when a line took his fancy, he would write it down in a black notebook. It was always with great reluctance that he made his way up the stairs to his small bed, his mind filled with golden wonder. The characters in the books he read were more vibrant than those in real life. They were vital and full of interest. He vowed that some day he would write a novel.

Already he knew that his novel would be set in Saint Petersburg and that the Royal prisoners would be characters in it.

Outside the printing works in the small garden, Pavlov began to dig the earth during his spare time. The black soil was dark and free. He raked manure with the earth and in the furrows planted his flowers and vegetables. Pavlov was pleased with his work. Flowers began to grow as the soft winds blew in from the Gulf of Finland.

"The earth is a wonderful thing," Pavlov often said. "Everything has its cycle. How can seeds endure the deep frost of winter and then burst open in spring? This is the stuff of poetry and novels."

Now the white nights of Saint Petersburg arrived. During the summer the city was suffused with light. By eleven in the evening the colours of the day had faded into pearl tones. There was always light in the east and then in the west. It never grew dark. Even the burden of war and sorrow seemed to lift during these bright months.

And yet there was turmoil at the parliament. Some wished that the great war would continue while the soviets, or workers' committees, cried out for an end to the war.

Vasily made his way to the Tauride Palace. By now he was familiar with all the key political actors who held the stage.

In July the streets were thronged with a half million people chanting "Down with the War!" A rising was crushed by the government. Lenin had been behind the move against the government. He was sought by the police, and had fled the city crossing the border into Finland.

Karensky, a well-educated lawyer, became Prime Minister. He had been elected to the Duma and wished to introduce many reforms; his mind was moderate and touched by compassion.

"Watch him. Follow him. He will not last," Dimitri told Vasily.

"Then what will happen?"

"It is in the hands of the gods."

Vasily continued to report the news from the city. One evening Dimitri called him aside.

"I have received some inside information. I believe that the Royal family are to be moved. Go to the village and sniff out the news. Here is some money. It will keep you a fortnight. Follow the train. Telegraph me of your movements and whereabouts."

"Do you trust me with such an undertaking?"

"You are good. You are young and strong. Who else can I turn to?"

Vasily returned to Tsarskoe Selo. It was high summer. The fields were green and the wind swept across the wide meadows, tossing the grass like waves. The silver birch were in delicate leaf and the village was filled with the scent of exotic flowers. He carried some tobacco for his favourite guard.

"Ah, my young friend. So you are in search of news?"

"As always," Vasily replied.

"Then you have come in time. But you must keep the news to yourself. The family are to be moved. Karensky has been here."

"When will they leave?"

"No one knows for certain."

"Where will they go?"

"No one knows that either. But a train is being got ready for them."

Vasily knew that he was on to a big story. The village had almost been abandoned by the revolution.

He handed the guard the tobacco he had brought with him.

"You are a good lad. Tonight I may have more news for you."

Vasily knew that he had to follow the story. He went to the post office and sent a telegram to Dimitri. He wrote in code. Then he made his way to the train station.

"Ah it is you," the stationmaster said.

"How are things since I saw you last?"

"I have new masters."

"There is a rumour at the palace that the family are to be moved."

The stationmaster turned pale and looked about him.

"Keep such matters to yourself. If this were reported in Saint Petersburg, the Soviets would take them in chains to the capital. Yes, they will be removed. Already the train is being prepared for them."

"Where is it bound?"

"East to the Urals. Perhaps they will be safe there."

"I must follow them. I must find out what happens."

They considered the position for some time. "Yes . . ." the stationmaster mused. "It could work."

"Have you a plan?" asked Vasily.

"Yes. Come with me."

Vasily followed the stationmaster to his room where he rummaged in an old cupboard. He took out a coat and trousers and a cap. Each of the items were thick with coal dust.

"It's just an idea . . . I know the engine driver and his friend. They may take you with them. You will have to stoke coal. Do you think you can do this?"

"Yes! Thank you. I will return early tomorrow morning."

The night of 13 August was very short. The scent of the flowers surrounded Tsarskoe Selo like an opiate.

Vasily walked in the gardens of Saint Catherine's Palace. The gardens were beginning to go wild. The hedges were untrimmed and weeds appeared on the paths. But the fountains worked and the water splashed softly from basin to basin. Vasily had grown to love the immense palace and hoped that whatever happened, it would be preserved.

Meanwhile, in the Alexander Palace, the prisoners were saying their last goodbyes to the members of the household and servants. All their belongings had been packed into a mountain of suitcases now piled in the large semi-circular hall. The children walked once more through the paths of the estate where they had spent their childhoods and their youth: the pond, the churches, the small coppices where they had played.

Karensky arrived at the palace at midnight. His task was delicate and dangerous. He had chosen three companies of soldiers to accompany the Royal family into exile and hoped that they could protect them.

The train was due at 1 a.m. Anxiously they waited for news of its arrival. The soldiers complained. They brushed past Nicholas as if he were of little importance. They refused him a cup of tea. Alexei's little spaniel, Joy, kept breaking loose and running through the hall. The four sisters waited patiently.

The family had often spoken of this moment. They looked at the unfriendly soldiers. Would they search their luggage for the jewels and precious stones they carried about their bodies?

Vasily did not sleep. He returned to the railway station. It was filled with soldiers.

"Who are you?" one of them asked.

"Reporting for duty, sir. I am apprenticed to the stoker. I've got to collect my gear at the stationmaster's office."

"Then hurry. The train could be along any moment."

Vasily entered the office and did not speak to the stationmaster, who was surrounded by soldiers. He put on the rough clothes, rubbed a sleeve across his forehead, and suitably soiled went back to the platform to wait. He looked down the line, which was bathed in mist.

The stationmaster's office was chaotic. It was difficult to clear the lines east.

At three in the morning luggage began to arrive from the palace. It was heaped on the platform. Vasily was surprised by the amount they were taking with them.

At long last the train emerged out of the morning mist. It bore strange flags and across it was written "Japanese Red Cross Mission".

The luggage was loaded on to the train.

"More like a travelling palace than a train," the driver said as he entered the railway station. He was large man with heavy jowls, a big stomach and a large wart on the end of his nose. He wiped his hand on an oily cloth.

"I have a lad here for you," the stationmaster said.

The train driver looked at Vasily. "Can you shovel coal?"

"Yes, sir," Vasily said.

"My mate Ilya will need someone to shovel coal. Go and meet him."

Vasily was excited at the adventure which lay ahead of him. He did not know where he was bound as he climbed on board the great engine.

His companion, Ilya, was a small ferret of a man, filled with energy and without a pick of surplus flesh.

"What are you doing here?" he asked.

"I've been sent to help shovel coal if necessary," Vasily said.

"Good. I've been shovelling coal for two days without a rest. Don't know where I've been. Don't know where I'm going either. I just shovel coal."

"Do you smoke?"

"When I can get tobacco. Tobacco is rationed now."

Vasily handed him his last pouch of tobacco. It was as valuable as gold to the stoker. He grinned a half-toothed grin. "You are a good fellow," he said.

Vasily jumped down from the engine, picked up a rag and began polishing a brass plate on the side of the train. Suddenly there was a flurry of movement.

The train had not been shunted to the platform. It stood some distance down the line. The Royal family had to walk along the side of the tracks to get to the first car. Vasily watched them walk towards him. He recognised them all. Nicholas, his wife Alexandra and their family. Alexandra leaned heavily on the arm of her husband. She found it difficult to walk.

A detachment of soldiers dressed in their new uniforms watched the Royal family walk to the train. At the head of the detachment stood Colonel Evgeny Kobylinsky.

They arrived at the first car. There were no steps. The men who had come with them lifted them on board. Vasily moved amongst them. He held out his hand towards Tatiana. She took it and he helped her aboard. She smiled at him.

"Thank you," she said.

He was struck by her simple dignity. Then he helped the others to board. He had not realised that so many were travelling into exile.

The train driver returned to the engine.

"Which way are we travelling, boss?" Ilya asked.

"None of your business," the driver snapped. "Your business is to shovel coal."

As the little man began to shovel coal, the train moved away from the beautiful village of Tsarskoe Selo without whistle or fanfare. Nobody waved goodbye as the train moved towards Saint Petersburg. It was 7:30 in the morning and the vast plains of Russia had never looked more beautiful.

CHAPTER 9

It was a glorious morning. The Royal family and its retainers looked back at the village growing smaller and smaller in the distance. Soon it would be a mound on the horizon; then it would disappear.

The train moved forward. Vasily knew that they were approaching Saint Petersburg. The furnace had been stoked and he could now look at the city. The train passed through it rapidly and soon they were moving east.

"Is it far to the Urals?" Vasily asked.

"Three, maybe four, days," the driver said.

The day grew warm and Vasily and the stoker began to bake in front of the furnace. The stoker sat down and opened a paper bag. He reached in and took out two boiled eggs and handed one to Vasily. They ate them with relish as they studied the countryside.

The driver spoke little. Despite the new revolution, he had little regard for the stoker whom he abused.

Meanwhile the Royal family were falling into a routine. Karensky had insisted that they be well treated.

The carriage was comfortable and the cook brought

them a light breakfast. As the day progressed, it grew stifling in the car and they had to open all the windows.

"I thought that we were going south," Olga remarked as she studied the flat landscape.

"I do not know," her father told her. "Even the guards do not seem to know where our destination lies."

"Then we are not going to the Livadia Palace," Maria, the prettiest daughter, said.

"Not for the moment. But things will sort themselves out."

They settled back into the long journey. They still felt secure. They had two valets, six chambermaids, three cooks and many others who would attend to their needs.

Behind them at some distance followed the second train. It carried the newly formed regiment of soldiers. Many of them argued about their assignments. They believed that Nicholas should be sent to prison.

"Perhaps we are helping him escape," one said.

"Yes," another agreed. "Will we let it be said that we helped Bloody Nicholas escape?"

They were all brave soldiers, tired of war and turmoil. Each one had been decorated for bravery.

Colonel Kobylinsky had to temper their anger.

"I have signed orders from Kerensky. You will get double pay for your work. Don't you see that they are going to Siberia? There is no escaping from the swamps."

"I have my suspicions," another soldier said.

They argued all through the long day and threw the windows open to draw in fresh air. The train was like a furnace and they sweated in their new uniforms.

The train passed through flat, even country which seemed to stretch on for ever. Here and there an onion dome indicated a village. To pass the time they played cards. Hour after hour the train passed across the plains, never reaching any horizon.

Then at evening they stopped. The doors were thrown open to let in the air and the heat was lessening and evening scents filled the carriages with their fragrance. Nicholas had indicated that he would like to walk in the fields.

Soldiers poured out of the carriages and lined up along the siding.

Nicholas and his family, together with their two dogs, walked through the fields. Vasily, eager to know what was going on, took a rag, jumped down and began polishing the brass.

The open space filled with laughter as the young women picked flowers. They seemed to belong in such simple places.

Suddenly, Alexei's little spaniel Joy broke loose. He ran down the track yelping and hid beneath the engine. Alexei followed him eagerly.

Vasily studied the young boy. He possessed fine skin and his hair was neatly combed. Vasily knew that he was a haemophiliac and his life was in constant danger. One bruise and he could die.

Alexei bent down and called to his dog.

"You are disobedient, Joy," he said. "Come here at once."

The little dog barked at him.

"I will fetch him for you," Vasily said, flopping down onto his hands and knees and crawling beneath the engine, where he grabbed the dog unceremoniously and handed him to Alexei.

"Thank you very much. Joy gets very excited. Can you drive this great train?" Alexei asked, looking at the engine.

"No. I stoke the coal and polish the brasses."

"Some day you will drive a train. If I were Tsar, then you could drive my train. We would go everywhere in Russia. I love to travel."

The conversation would have continued but Tatiana called to him.

"That is my sister Tatiana," he said. "She's very bossy. Again, thank you very much."

He turned and left. Vasily watched him enter the carriage with his father. Then the doors were shut.

Vasily climbed aboard and the train started again.

"You should have spat on him," the train driver said when he entered the train. His voice was angry and his face sullen.

"He has done nothing to me," Vasily answered tartly.

"They should be all shot, the whole lot of them."

Night fell. The sky grew dark. Vasily climbed on to the coal bunker and found a place at the end where he could sleep. He bedded down for the night on a rough mattress which belonged to the stoker. The train passed across the endless plains.

When he awoke he looked at the sun's position in the sky. He had slept late. He rubbed the sleep from his eyes and gazed over the rim of the coal carriage. Habitation seemed remote.

They were moving further and further away from civilisation. As they moved east he noted the change in the people working in the fields. They seemed planted and solid with sad faces which reflected the harsh realities of life.

"Did you sleep?" the driver asked.

"Yes, I slept soundly."

"Then you can stoke the coal. Let Ilya sleep. I leave the train at the next station."

No word passed between them. Vasily took the wide shovel and threw coal into the depths of the furnace.

The train moved quickly across the open plain before coming to a halt at a railway station. The station was surrounded by a huddle of miserable huts. Pigs roamed the streets and there was a stench of filth in the air. The soldiers rushed from their carriages in order to guard the train. The peasants looked on with passive eyes.

The Colonel entered the telegraph office and sent a coded message to Saint Petersburg. It stated that they were moving towards the Urals and had encountered no opposition.

They took a new driver on board and a half an hour later set out again.

On the third day they had their first view of the Urals. The mountains rose majestically out of the flat plains. They were the divide between east and west. Beyond the mountains lay Asia and the vast tract of Siberia.

Vasily looked at the mountain range in wonder, and observed as slowly the mountains came closer. When the train approached some small hills, they began to move through the barrier between east and west. The trains slowed down as they moved up the gradient. The passengers watched the chasms gather about them where the rock had been hewn away to make way for the tracks. Tenacious pines and larch clung to the sides of the mountains.

At a certain point the train began to gather speed again. They were descending towards Asia. The air grew cooler as they passed through Ekaterinburg in the early hours of the morning. Light poured out of the east and gave a brilliance to the land. They passed onwards through a flat countryside which seemed to go on forever. Then they entered the taiga, an area of boggy woodland, with Siberian poplars, Scotch pines, alder and birch. Here and there they could see a village or some signs of agriculture.

"There is no escape from here," Ilya told him. "I always feel lost. It is wild country and it goes on forever. Further north are the prison camps. They need no walls – swamps are the walls."

"Have you seen the prisoners?"

"Yes, I've seen them. I've stoked all kinds of trains: timber trains, coal trains, prison trains. The prison trains were the worst."

Now Vasily looked at the majestic trees, growing tall and steady by the tracks in a new light. When the train stopped in the middle of the vast forest, Nicholas and his children stepped down from the carriage to take some exercise. By now Vasily knew each one of them. They were always in good humour and their behaviour was courteous.

Vasily felt a growing pity for them. He possessed his freedom, yet despite their luxurious carriages they were like birds in a golden cage. He documented his impressions in a notebook which he carried in his pocket. Each evening as he prepared for bed, he tried to commit his thoughts to paper. The pages were smudged and the writing flawed but he had written down his impressions.

It was near midnight on 17 August when the train crawled slowly into Tyumen. All the passengers were weary after their journey. Lights burned along the platform in a ghostly fashion. Suddenly the soldiers poured out of their train. They hurried along the platform and sealed off the entrances.

Across from the station stood a dock. Here ships and boats which plied the Tura river lay at anchor. It was a mysterious place at night time, with voices calling out in the darkness and sailors passing between the lights and half-lights. The lamps and moonlight cast a silver path on the river. A boat with burning lanterns moved into mid-stream.

The *Rouss* lay moored close at hand. It was a river steamer which would take them upstream to the town of Tobolsk.

Immediately the soldiers began to drag luggage from the compartments. The Royal family boarded the *Rouss* and tried to sleep.

Vasily also left the train, having said goodbye to the stoker who grinned and waved to him. Ilya had travelled half Russia yet he had rarely moved from the space between the coal car and the face of the furnace.

Vasily walked out into the street. The place was dimly lit. The buildings were mostly built out of timber except for a few central buildings of stone. He realised he was far from the elegance of Saint Petersburg.

He entered a sailors' tavern. It was a dark place lit by naked bulbs. It smelt of tar and acrid sweat. The cast of most of the faces were Asiatic.

"Well, lad, where do you come from?" one of the sailors asked.

"Saint Petersburg."

"It's a long journey from Saint Petersburg to Tyumen. All of four days they say."

"Yes. Four days," Vasily replied.

"And where are you bound?"

"To where the *Rouss* is bound."

"That would be Tobolsk. That is two days' journey from here."

"I am willing to work my way on board a steamer."

"What is your experience?"

"I stoked coal all the way from Saint Petersburg."

"Captain Karl should take you. He is a drunkard. He can rarely keep a crew."

"Where is Captain Karl?"

"Down at the end of the bar drinking vodka," the sailors nodded in the captain's direction.

Vasily approached the formidable captain, one of the most gigantic men he had ever seen in his life.

"Do you want to take a stoker on board, Captain Karl?" he asked rather timidly.

The Captain looked at him through drunken eyes.

"I need a man, not a lad," he replied in a garrulous voice.

"Do you need someone to write letters?" Vasily asked quickly.

"That I do. If you keep the log for me and write some letters, you can come on board. We leave in three maybe four days' time."

"Can I sleep on board the steamer in the meantime? I have no lodgings."

"Ah, son. We will find a bunk for you in some corner or other. The Chinese cook will show you around the place. Watch him or he'll chop your fingers off for soup!"

He let out a roar of laughter which shook the tavern.

Vasily felt that he should purchase a dagger; he felt threatened in the place. Outside in the fresh air he made his way along the quay and found the steamer. It was an ugly tub rusting at the seams.

He climbed on board and found the cook.

"Captain Karl. He mad with drink?" the Chinese cook asked.

"Yes, he is drunk."

"Soon he will be full drunk and then there will be a fight. He terrible man in fight. He mad you know."

After some exploration Vasily finally found a berth in the lifeboat. He lined it with some rough sisal bags and slept soundly.

When he woke in the morning he could see the port more clearly. It was well situated and high on the bank of a long and wide river. The sun was touching it with light. The *Rouss* was just beginning to move away from the dock. He watched it navigate into the river and then push against the water. Soon it was under full steam. It was followed by two other vessels which carried the servants and baggage. Vasily watched them pass down the river Tura.

In the meantime he had much work to catch up on. He purchased a new notebook and transcribed his notes on to clean paper. He made two copies following the advice he had received from Pavlov. Having put them in order, he parcelled one up and brought it to the post office.

Vasily posted it to Dimitri for safe keeping. He filled his days sitting on board the ship reading books he had purchased in town.

The Chinese cook called to him from his post.

"You growing boy. You eat plenty," he said, handing him a dish of meat and vegetables.

"Where is Captain Karl?" Vasily asked.

"He in prison. He cool off."

Three days later Captain Karl appeared, sober. He checked the grain cargo, paid his harbour fee and hauled in the anchor. He called Vasily to his cabin.

"Read for me," he said, handing him a travel book.

Gazing down river Captain Karl listened as Vasily read the voyages of Captain Cook. Captain Karl never spoke while Vasily recounted the story.

"You read well," he said when he had finished. "I like someone who can read to me. See that the Chinaman feeds you well. He is a good fellow."

"He bad on land but great on river. He never drink on river. He keep much to himself. Strange man, Captain Karl, but I like him," the Chinese cook said the first afternoon when they were sitting together.

That evening they anchored at Pokrovskoe.

"This is an interesting place. Rasputin was born in this village. I knew him on the river. Filthy fellow. Drank too much like myself, then he went to Saint Petersburg and kept the company of royalty," Captain Karl said.

Vasily was excited to see where Rasputin had lived. Everyone he met had some story to tell about Rasputin.

"I was at Tsarskoe Selo when the soldiers burned his body in the forest," Vasily told him.

"He was an evil influence on Alexandra. He softened her mind. I often saw him in this village rolling home drunk. He had family here."

Vasily went ashore. The village consisted of several streets of spacious wooden houses. They were ornamented with carved and painted window frames which added charm to the desolate landscape.

Pokrovskoe was surrounded by marshlands. Conifers grew on high ground. The town was dominated by a large white church with a gilded dome.

The captain had indicated Rasputin's house. It was a two-storeyed building overlooking the village. Vasily found it hard to believe that the man who had been assassinated at Saint Petersburg and who had bought the Empire to its knees had come from a remote place in the middle of a vast marshland.

He savoured the mystery of the locality before returning to the steamer. They anchored in Pokrovskoe for the night. Vasily sat on the deck and looked at the village. The lights had come on in the windows and there was some singing in the streets. A fight broke out – then there was silence.

Vasily watched as one by one the stars appeared in the sky. They glittered like diamonds. He pulled the tarpaulin closer about him and fell asleep.

The next day they set off for Tobolsk; the great river carried them smoothly forward. The Captain showed Vasily his maps. The river system was like a network across the land.

"Follow the river and it would take you to the Kara Sea," he said.

It was a vast area, empty and swampy except for the trees and wild animals. In the far north lay the tundra. It was a pleasant time of year on the river. Fishermen in frail boats cast their nets into the water. Here and there peasants were gathering hay.

"The very end of the world," Captain Karl said. "This is the Tsars' great prison. All over this vast land are prisons. No one ever escapes."

That evening at sunset they reached the ancient town of Tobolsk. It stood on an elevation and was marked by an old fortress and the onion bulbs of the city churches.

They docked at the wharf.

"This is a backwater," Captain Karl said. "Are you sure you wish to stay here? It's not too late to stay with me. I will show you all Siberia."

"Thank you" Vasily replied. "But I cannot come with you, I am following a story."

"Then you will need work to survive in this miserable place. I can get you work. Follow me."

He brought him to a merchant he knew who dealt in furs.

"Give the lad work, Fedor. He writes well. He will keep an account of all your skins."

The merchant studied Vasily critically from narrow eyes. He had Asiatic features and a lined face.

"Very well. I will pay him. He will not starve. I need an honest fellow. The last person I employed ran away with all my best furs. The world is filled with rogues."

"Have Nicholas and his family arrived?" Vasily asked.

"Yes some days ago. They are in 'Freedom House'."

Captain Karl began to laugh "'Freedom House'. And where is 'Freedom House'?"

"In Freedom Street," the merchant replied matter-of-factly.

"People have gone mad with this new freedom." Captain Karl observed. "Let them wait a little longer. Soon they will wish that Nicholas was back on the throne."

"Such talk is dangerous," Fedor said.

"I don't care. I know these fellows who will run our new world. They are rascals. But you take good care of Vasily," Captain Karl told Fedor. He said goodbye to the boy and turned and left the office.

"Come with me and I will show you the operation," the merchant said.

He led him along the quay and showed him where he would live. It was a comfortable loft at the end of a great warehouse.

"Do you think will you will be happy here?" Fedor asked.

113

"Yes. I'm sure I will be happy."

"Good. Can you drive a lorry?"

"No."

"Then I will show you some day. It is important to know such things. One thing's for sure. You will never be cold here. You have the finest furs in Siberia to wrap about you," he laughed.

He left Vasily to settle into his new quarters. He would live here for eight months. By the end of that time he would know much about the fur trade. He would be an expert on the smell and texture of fur.

Vasily spent two days with Captain Karl, helping him get his papers in order before moving into his quarters above the great warehouse.

The next day he began to explore Tobolsk.

The streets were dusty, the houses chiefly constructed of whitewashed wood. Window boxes filled with flowers added a dash of colour to the city. Vasily listened to the conversation of the people. Everyone was speaking about the Imperial visitors to the city, particularly the women. They spoke of the clothes worn by the Imperial family and the way in which their hair was cut.

"Alexandra is much older than Nicholas. And I believe that she needs a wheelchair," one woman said.

"It rumoured that she makes the children's beds."

"Fancy an empress making her children's beds. I just can't believe it."

"And you would think the girls would have airs. Not at all. I believe that they nursed the wounded soldiers in Saint Petersburg."

"Imagine. It's hard to believe."

"Live and learn. I've seen them take the sun on the balcony of the governor's house each evening."

"So have I. They look very normal."

"Even Alexei. He's a bleeder you know. A woman I met explained it all to me. He bleeds inside. Rasputin could cure him."

"That blaggard. He was a queer one. There are stories I could tell you, but I'm a Christian lady so I won't."

"Do tell me more; you can trust me."

"Well . . . he was in Tobolsk once. You know that."

"Yes . . . "

"Well, perhaps you've noticed that certain respectable ladies in the city have children who bear a striking resemblance to Rasputin."

"You don't tell me!"

"Indeed I do. Keep your eyes open. And there is more but I'm a charitable lady who keeps her thoughts to herself . . . there are rumours that Alexandra and Rasputin were more than friends."

"Well I never."

The Imperial family had already become the subject of coarse gossip.

Eventually Vasily made his way to the governor's house. It was a spacious place, large, white and two-storeyed, with balconies on the second floor.

"Are they all housed here?" Vasily asked one of the soldiers.

"No. Some of the servants are at Kornilov's house which is across the street."

The soldier pointed out the house to him, then studied him carefully.

"Have I not seen you somewhere before?"

"Perhaps. I was on board the train which brought the family to Tyumen. I worked on board a steamer which carried me here and now I work for a fur trader."

"You get around."

"I am interested in the family and their fate."

"Aren't we all? Still, I don't wish to spend the whole of the winter here. I believe that they will ship them to England. They are related to the Royal family. Surely they will take them. Such arrangements are being made at present, at least that is what I heard."

Vasily had studied the history of the Romanovs and he knew that they were related to most of the Royal houses in Europe. It seemed clear to him that they would eventually be taken abroad. But nagging doubts remained in his mind. Siberia was a prison and with the advent of winter they would be snowed-in, unable to move anywhere until the ice melted.

That night Vasily passed through the city on his way to the warehouse. Electric lights were glowing in the windows as he passed by the 'House of Freedom'.

Vasily had come halfway across Russia following the story, tracing the fortunes of Nicholas and his family. He wondered if his story would soon end as he continued through the dusty streets, making his way along the quay. There were lights on in some of the steamers. He opened the warehouse and let himself in and climbed to his loft.

It was dark, and bright stars arched across Siberia.

CHAPTER 10

Vasily was standing on the pier when the jailers arrived. By now it was late autumn. He studied both men. Pankratov was a small man with thick glasses who had been sent to supervise the prisoners. He had spent many years in Siberia and he had no reason to like the Tsar. Yet despite his low stature he possessed some dignity.

He was accompanied by Nikolsky, who was tall and broad. His face was heavy and thick hair fell about his shoulders.

Vasily was helping a hunter with his pelts. The hunter had arrived from the north and they were carrying them to the warehouse. He was a morose man who lived in the forests during the winter. "I do not like them," he said, nodding in the direction of the two jailers. "They are bent on evil."

It took Vasily a day to discover who they were.

They had been sent by the Provincial government to take command of the Tsar and his family. He learned that both had spent many years as Siberian prisoners.

Nikolsky hated the Tsar. "He is to blame for all my

troubles," he said in drink. "But now I'll show him who is in charge. Nikolsky."

Both men sat in the tavern and ate a meal. Vasily was present with the hunter.

Pankratov noted that Vasily was reading a newspaper.

"You. Can you read?" he asked.

"Yes. I also write."

"Good. I noted you working on the docks. When the post arrives by river steamer, bring it directly to me. I will pay you well."

Vasily was delighted with the offer. Now he could get close to the governor's house.

He followed Pankratov and Nikolsky to their quarters which faced the governor's house.

"The prisoners have taken over the prison," Vasily thought to himself.

"You come tomorrow and show me this town. We will be here for some time and it is important that I become acquainted with it," Pankratov said.

He was the gentler and more refined of the two.

Vasily wondered what was happening in the governor's house across the road. Some strangers had visited the town. They were too talkative and had vague plans to rescue the family. But Tobolsk had its spies and informers. They had quickly been captured and dispatched to Saint Petersburg.

Vasily had established himself with the merchant. He had filled in many forms for him and cleared up the warehouse. Everything was in order and ready to be dispatched to the great cities in Russia and Europe. He had even succeeded in learning how to drive the lorry.

Fedor had explained to him how the engine worked.

"You're a clever lad," he told him. "You will go far. You stay with me and I will make you a rich man."

Now he had time to set down his thoughts on paper. His loft had an electric light and he had secured paper. He drew up the plans of Tobolsk and set down the names of Nicholas's retinue.

He felt pity for the prisoners. They did not know how much the world had changed. Vasily could see that the war had changed everything.

The Imperial family still played out the old rituals up at the governor's house. The servants copied out the menus on paper with Nicholas's seal. They went about their traditional roles as if they were in the Alexander Palace, oblivious to the fact that history was changing about them.

It was changing in the persons of Pankratov and Nikolsky.

Next morning Vasily was ready to bring Pankratov on a tour to the city. Pankratov was interested in everything: the churches, the great buildings, and the tundra beyond the limits of the town. It was clear to him that the only escape could be by river. He would set guards on the pier when they returned.

"And now you come with me to the governor's house," he told Vasily. "I must meet Nicholas."

They set off together, Vasily several inches taller than the little man. They passed the soldiers, entered the house and mounted the stairs to the first floor. Vasily studied everything. His eyes were hungry for details. Here he had reached the very heart of the mystery.

"Announce me to Citizen Romanov," Pankratov said politely to Nicholas's valet.

After some time Nicholas arrived. He was dressed in the simple khaki shirt of a soldier and wore a rough trousers, which were frayed at the knees. He received Pankratov with a certain amount of grace. They spoke for some time about general matters.

"Have you any requests?" Pankratov asked.

"Could you allow me to saw some logs of wood?"

Pankratov looked at him with a startled expression.

"Simple logs of wood. I like the exercise. And I can build up a stock of fuel for the winter."

"Very well. It can be arranged."

"And could my family and I walk in the town and the countryside? It would be good for our health."

"No. I am afraid I cannot grant such a freedom. I am responsible for your safety."

The refusal stung Nicholas, who turned his head away.

"How is your son Alexei?" Pankratov enquired.

"Very good. He has not been this well for quite some time."

Pankratov now broached a delicate point.

"I am afraid that I will have to censor your letters. I have received my orders. I know it is an intrusion on your privacy but it must be done."

"What can we do at Tobolsk that would shake the government?" Nicholas observed caustically. "We are prisoners."

"I'm sorry. These are my orders."

"Yes, well I do not like them."

"They have to be obeyed."

With that the two men bowed and Pankratov turned on his heels. Just then the four girls passed them. As always they wore simple dresses. Vasily was struck by their beauty and composure.

Alexei followed. He stood for a moment and he and Vasily looked at one another.

"How are you?" Alexei asked.

"Very well."

"How is life on the great train?"

"It is far away. I now work in a warehouse."

"I wish I could work with you. Here I am restrained. I would like to walk with you in the fresh air. I'm sure that there is much you could teach me."

"How is your dog?"

"Oh, Joy is well."

His sisters called him. Alexei excused himself. "I hope I see you again." With that he followed his sisters down the corridor.

"You know each other?" Pankratov asked incredulously.

"I met him once. I rescued his dog."

They returned to the house across the street. Pankratov was agitated. "Nicholas has no confidence in me," he began. "I could see it in his eyes."

"But why not let them walk in the country?" Vasily asked boldly.

"And be assassinated? Do you realise how hated the Romanovs are? The people call for their blood. We are inundated with letters of hate in Saint Petersburg. Many of them come from Tobolsk. I know what I am doing. While I am here, they are protected."

Pankratov sat down and began to write a report. His face was intent. He wrote carefully, taking pride in each letter.

"Ah," he said after the first paragraph, "I think I have got it correct."

He looked at Vasily.

"While I write, you go through Nicholas's post. See if there is anything of a rebellious nature in it."

"The Tsar's post?"

"Yes."

Vasily took the first envelope and with trembling hands drew out the letter. It carried the Imperial eagles on top. He felt that he was preying on someone's innermost thoughts. He was struck by the easy style in which the letters were written. He continued to read the letters. They had a common touch and were without guile.

Then he turned to the letters of the Tsarina. Alexandra's letters were filled with notes of sadness.

He particularly remembered one which would haunt him later in life.

"Yes. The past is over, I thank God for all I had and was given . . . My youth is over. My near and dear are all far, far away. I am surrounded by their photographs and possessions . . . a robe, slippers, a saucer, an icon . . . How old I am."

He committed such sentences to memory and later wrote them down.

"Well, did you find anything to note?"

"No. I can find no secret plot here. They are simple letters, pleasant and familiar."

"Good. Seal them and bring them to the post office. Thank goodness I found someone who can read and write."

Vasily passed through the town on his way to the post office. At several corners stood soldiers recently returned from the war. Many of them were wounded. He listened to their talk. One could always judge the temper of the times from such conversations.

"Nicholas cost me a leg and an eye. I have no love for the tyrant. Shoot him, I say."

"Members of his court strut about the town. What do they know of hunger or the trenches? I was sent to the

Front with a pick axe, nothing more. Kill them I say. They have blood on their hands."

But there were others who thought that the Imperial family were sacred figures, chosen by God. They believed that ill fortune would descend on those who harmed them.

Vasily posted the letters and returned to the office. When Pankratov had no further work for him, he went to the warehouse. A steamer had arrived from Tyumen which would carry much of the stock south before winter set in. He stood on the pier while the precious pelts were loaded. Bale by bale they were lowered into the hold. Vasily ticked them off against a list he carried.

"I will travel with the precious cargo as far as Saint Petersburg," the merchant said. "Take care of the warehouse while I am away. I shall return in three weeks' time."

"Very well," said Vasily. "I will take good care of things while you are away."

"And I will bring you news from the great city and some books."

Vasily watched the steamer with its plume of black smoke thresh its way into midstream, before heading south.

Vasily wished that he were on board. Winter would soon descend on Siberia and all contact with the outside world would be severed.

He returned to the warehouse. It was now almost empty. He could expect a few more trappers from the north and that would bring the season to an end. The trappers were running against time; soon cold winds would bear down on them and the dealing in pelts would end until next spring when the ice thawed.

By now Vasily had filled several notebooks with

writing. Again, he painstakingly copied each notebook and posted it to Saint Petersburg.

Dimitri had written him a letter of praise.

"Your style improves. It is simple and you understand how the smallest detail can convey great feeling. Continue to read. P.S. Are you becoming a Royalist?"

It was true. Vasily's feelings for Nicholas and his family had changed enormously. He had read their letters and had been in their presence. He had even delivered letters to Nicholas himself. The girls and Alexei had talked to him, while the Empress remained aloof. On one occasion he had played cards with the Tsar and the guards.

But times were changing faster than Vasily could imagine.

One evening he sat down to read as usual. He had acquired a new volume by Pushkin and had been looking forward to reading it.

Suddenly the door of his loft was flung open. A man with a revolver appeared. Vasily had seen him disembark two days earlier at the pier. The man put his fingers to his lips. "Listen and listen very closely," he hissed.

Vasily nodded.

The man began to speak. "I have come from Saint Petersburg. Time is running out. Lenin has taken over the city. He despises Nicholas. We have little time to act. If the family is to escape, the time is now."

"Is it possible?" asked Vasily.

"Of course it is possible. Why do you think Karensky sent them here? They can escape into China and make their way to Europe from there."

He took out a map and showed Vasily the railway

line running all the way to Vladivostock on the coast of
the Sea of Japan. Along the way were red marks.

"What do these represent?" Vasily asked.

"They are sympathisers. They would die for
Nicholas. But time is running out. We must get both
himself and his son out of Tobolsk."

"How can I help?"

"You deliver the post each day. Take this plan to
Nicholas. Let him study it. You are familiar with Captain
Karl. He will take them down river by steamer. We
have horses ready to take them across country from
there. There are several monasteries along the way
which will hide them."

"What if I do not help?"

"Then the blood of Nicholas is on your hands."

The bleak statement frightened him. It was up to
him to help.

"Very well, I can only try."

"Remember. We have only a fortnight. The weather
is closing in on us. It's now or never. If we do not
make a dash for it now, we will never succeed."

The stranger left him with the map and some notes.
When he had gone, Vasily began to consider the
situation. Once he had cursed Nicholas; now he was
about to help him escape.

The next morning he arrived at the headquarters.

Nikolsky was in a rage. Wine had been brought
from Saint Petersburg for Nicholas and his family.

"I will not have them spoiled. Take the wine and
throw it in the river. I was not pampered with Royal
wine while I rotted in one of his Siberian jails. Russia
starves and citizen Romanov orders wine from Saint
Petersburg."

After much argument, the wine which had arrived at

the office was placed on a cart. Nikolsky set off for the river. There in a dramatic gesture he knocked the tops off the bottles and poured the wine into the river. It was a mean demonstration of his power and Vasily detested him. He was arrogant and had little feeling for Nicholas or his family. On many occasions he had observed him humiliate the Tsar. He had knocked a plate of soup onto the Emperor's lap.

When Nikolsky had gone with the wine, Vasily stood up and stretched.

"I will deliver the mail," he said. He took the few letters which had arrived and crossed over the road to the governor's house.

The guards were lax on that day. They were only concerned with the fate of the wine.

Vasily passed directly into the house and walked up the stairs. He knocked on a door and Nicholas bade him enter.

"Ah, Vasily. Have you good or bad news for me?"

Vasily closed the door and secured it. Then he went over to the desk and handed Nicholas the map and the notes.

"These were given to me by a friend from Saint Petersburg. You must study them quickly and make up your mind. He says that you have a fortnight left before the winter closes in."

"You would place your life in danger for me and my family?" Nicholas asked.

"I do not wish to see you harmed," Vasily replied.

He took the letters Nicholas had written and left the house. He carried them to Pankratov, who read them rapidly.

"Trivial matters," he said, ordering Vasily to close and post them.

That afternoon Vasily returned to the warehouse. The mysterious stranger from Saint Petersburg was waiting for him.

"Well? Did you give him the plans?"

"Yes. He will study them tonight."

"Make sure he does. Time is running out."

That night as he lay in bed Vasily wondered what decision Nicholas had reached.

From the window of his loft he could see the governor's house. The lights burned in the Tsar's room.

Nicholas had gathered his family about him. Though Alexandra's hair had grown grey and she walked with more and more difficulty, she was still a woman of great beauty. The daughters, all dressed alike, sat on chairs. The group huddled about the fire and Nicholas explained in hushed tones the plan of escape to them.

"You must flee, Father. This is your chance. There are monasteries all over Siberia where you can take refuge. They will not harm us."

"I have given this much thought," Nicholas said. "I cannot not leave Russia during its time of troubles. I will remain; if necessary I will die here. The country bleeds; it does not befit the Tsar to run away."

"Very good," said Alexandra. "We will abide by your decision."

Then it was time for their night prayer. Kneeling before a sacred icon, the family recited the psalms and retired to bed.

The next day Vasily visited Nicholas. The plans were returned.

"It is not possible," Nicholas said. "I cannot leave my family. I cannot leave Russia."

Vasily could not believe his ears, but carried the news to the man from Saint Petersburg, who was waiting in the warehouse.

"It is over," he said simply. "Nicholas has made a foolish decision. I fear that there will be a dreadful outcome to all this."

The next day he boarded the river steamer and left Tobolsk. Vasily stood on the pier and waved him off.

A cold wind blew across the wide expanse of water. Soon the snow would follow. Vasily returned to the warehouse. He knew that things were about to take a bad turn.

CHAPTER 11

Winter arrived. They winds wheeled down from Siberia. They were bitterly cold. The ground grew hard as iron and the frost set in. Then the snows followed, falling on the vast empty land, making movement almost impossible except for the expert traveller.

The snow settled on the onion domes of churches and on the rooftops. It piled up on the streets and stood deep about the forest's edges.

Snow fell persistently for a week. Tobolsk was isolated. Only the church bells gave a sense of life to the place.

The water of the great river froze, first close to the banks, then gradually the whole river froze. Two steamers were trapped for the winter. November was the beginning of the bad times.

News arrived that Karensky had left Saint Petersburg and that there had been a revolution in Moscow. A new Soviet government had been elected and Lenin had been made chairman.

"It is bad news," Vasily told the merchant, who had returned from Saint Petersburg.

He had come overland and had been several weeks late.

"Why do you say that?"

"I have been in Saint Petersburg. I have heard Lenin speak. He hates Nicholas and his family."

"What will happen then?"

"I do not know, but I fear for the lives of the Romanovs."

By now Vasily's life had settled into a routine. He had changed. Another year older, he grew restless. There was very little for him to do in the warehouse. He had purchased a gun and frequently went shooting at the edge of the forest. At times he ventured into the forest, a mysterious place in winter. There was always the danger that he might be set upon by hungry wolves, but somehow this danger attracted him.

It also gave him time to reflect. He was particularly distraught by a letter which Alexandra had written. More than the others, it expressed her sadness and grief:

"One by one all earthly things slip away, houses and possessions ruined, friends vanished. One lives from day to day. But God is in all and nature never changes."

In another letter she had written:

"There are such moonlit nights, it must be ideal on the hills. But my poor unfortunates can only pace up and down the narrow yard . . . I make everything now. Nicholas's trousers are torn and darned, the girls' under-linen in rags."

These words stirred Vasily greatly and he schemed to help them escape.

Whenever the post arrived and had been read, he carried it to the governor's house. He was now familiar with the family. Sometimes he spoke with Alexei. He told him that he frequently had gone hunting in the forest.

Alexei listened to his stories with a sense of wonder.

"I would go with you but I am not permitted. I grow weary of this house."

He noted that the girls' clothes were indeed becoming shabby. Yet they were always in good humour. He knew their names and ages. Olga was twenty-two, Tatiana was twenty, Maria eighteen and Anastasia sixteen. They were always together and they were always friendly.

In December the full force of winter hit Tobolsk. Temperatures dropped far below freezing point. Nothing could keep out the cold. In the governor's house, Nicholas and his family shivered. They gathered about the small fire and tried to keep themselves warm.

At night, wrapped up in his warm bed of furs, reading a book, Vasily often thought of them and his heart filled with pity.

Christmas was approaching, bringing some excitement to Tobolsk. People prepared trees and decorated them with candles and coloured paper. There was a sense of expectation in the air.

On Christmas morning the bells pealed out over Tobolsk. They filled the alleyways and the streets with their sonorous echoes.

Vasily watched the Imperial family cross the public garden for Mass. The privilege was often afforded them. He followed them at a respectful distance.

He entered the church and pushed his way up the side aisle. He took delight in the scent of incense, the colour of the icons which were painted on the walls, the deep voices of the cantors. His mother had taught him how to read the icons. Their colour and texture were full of meaning and mystery for him.

It happened at the end of Mass, a mistake which would have serious repercussions.

The deacon had just begun to chant prayers for the Royal Family. His deep voice filled the church.

"Let us pray for their Excellencies the Sovereign Emperor and the Sovereign Empress and their children."

"A long life," the congregation called out.

Such pro-Royalist declarations amounted to treason for the new government. Some of the soldiers who stood at the back of the church became angry.

"They are no longer the Royal family," one of them called. "They are common Romanovs now."

The family moved out of the church with their eyes averted. The congregation permitted them to pass through, some blessing themselves.

Pankratov and Nikolsky were furious at the priest. He was called before them.

"We have prisons right across Siberia. Perhaps a night in one might cool your Imperialistic fervour," Nikolsky ranted.

"It was a mistake," the priest stammered.

"It was no mistake! The Romanovs will suffer for this folly."

From then on, the family were refused permission to visit the church.

"They take everything from us," Alexandra complained.

Nicholas remained patient. He always remained calm even in the most trying circumstances. Soon after the incident, some of the soldiers turned hostile. Vasily listened to them argue in the tavern.

"We owe him nothing. We are now free. He brought about this terrible war. He should be shot."

Most of them agreed.

"And why should we take orders from Kobylinsky? Let us set up a soldiers' committee. He is one of them. He belongs to the old order."

Shortly thereafter a soldiers' committee was established. They ordered Nicholas to remove the epaulets he always wore. Though he felt humiliated, he obeyed.

January passed into February. The weather was monotonous. It was still bitterly cold. One day the soldiers' committee decided that Pankratov and Nikolsky should resign. The tide was turning against the Imperial family.

"The revolution begins to eat its young," the merchant said to Vasily when he heard the news. "I do not like it. I do not like it at all. They are blaggards – uneducated poltroons I call them."

"Keep your words to yourself," Vasily warned. "These are dangerous times."

But the merchant was right. As spring approached, orders came from Moscow that the old soldiers should resign. These soldiers, who had belonged to another Russia, and who had accompanied the Romanovs on their train journey from Tsarskoe Selo, came secretly and took their leave of Nicholas.

He looked from one to another with tears in his eyes. Had he asked them, they would have said they would still die for him.

From a bank of snow they had built inside the fence the family watched them leave. This bank of snow had been a great source of pleasure to them, particularly Alexei, who loved to slide down the even slope on a sleigh.

Now the soldiers' committee, which had been created from the ordinary soldiers, ordered the slope to be demolished. Vasily watched Nicholas and his family grow depressed at their treatment. They were regarded with more and more disrespect and grew pale and sickly. The faces of the girls grew gaunt. It soon became almost impossible to gain access to them. Gradually they were losing contact with the world.

Everywhere the signs of spring were evident. The river thawed and the ice broke into great chunks which moved slowly towards the sea. The frost lost its grip on the earth and people began to dig their small gardens. Buds appeared on the trees and birds began to return from the south.

A few days later, Vasily was standing at the pier when he noticed Captain Karl's steamer approach. It was the first to arrive at port since the ice had begun to thaw. On board the ship were the new soldiers sent to guard Nicholas and his family. Vasily watched them pass in disorder.

"I would shoot them," Captain Karl said. "They have no discipline. They abused my passengers, particularly the women. I had to force myself to restrain my temper. These are dangerous times."

"Are you a Royalist, Captain Karl?" Vasily asked point blank one evening when they were alone.

"Of course I am. You need an emperor to govern. Politicians are blaggards. They are not to be trusted."

They sat together in the cabin. Vasily told him how he had passed the winter and how he had visited Nicholas and his family on several occasions.

"Things are changing, Vasily. They are changing every day. Do you know how to use a revolver?"

"I can use a rifle."

"Take this revolver then. You may need to use it. But keep it hidden. If you must practise, practise in the forests."

"Do you think there will be another attempt to save the family?"

"I do not know. Things grow more difficult, as I said. We may be able to mount one more rescue bid."

But the young man could see that Captain Karl did not feel very confident. Vasily said goodbye and returned to the warehouse. He often looked at the governor's house at night time. and wondered what was going on behind the windows. The lights were on. Now the family's privacy had been breached, the soldiers kept guard inside as well as outside the house.

Vasily often slipped into the tavern where the soldiers drank and listened to their conversation. It was raw and obscene.

"Soon they will be on army rations – and why not. They are common folk like us. They should sup as we do."

"Rightly so. Jack is now as good as his master."

At times it was hard for Vasily to contain his anger. He could only sit and listen.

The Romanovs, once the most powerful family in Europe, were virtual prisoners and received little respect. When the money to pay the soldiers ran out, they were paid from money set aside for Nicholas and his family. For the first time in over three hundred years the Romanovs were poor. When the cook could no longer purchase food in the shops, a telegram arrived which placed them on soldiers' rations.

The family gathered together. They knew that they could no longer pay their servants.

"But what will they do, Papa?" Anastasia asked.

"They will leave us. They must return to Saint Petersburg. Some of them have brought their families with them."

"And what will happen them when they return?"

"I do not know."

There was a note of desperation in his voice.

The family now went hungry. They could no longer afford coffee or butter.

"Serves them right," one of the young soldiers said in the market place. An old woman hit him with her bag.

"You are a young pup," she said.

"I could shoot you," the young soldier said arrogantly.

"Then shoot me," she said, facing him down.

He turned away sheepishly.

Now the people of Tobolsk began to send food parcels to the governor's house. The soldiers realised the family still retained the respect of the people.

"At least they will eat well," an old woman said as she laboured up the hill towards the house. "Imagine, the anointed one of God going without food. It's a disgrace! Everything will come to a bad end."

With the approach of spring the days grew longer and only patches of snow lay in secluded places to remind them of the winter and Alexandra often sat on the balcony and took the sun. She had aged rapidly and no longer had the bearing of an Empress. She was now a disabled woman who was frequently pushed about in a wheelchair by her husband. She had longed for the spring. The winter had brought the family close together and she was proud of her children. Perhaps with the coming of Easter there might be a miracle. She often prayed for a miracle. One day Alexei began to bleed. He had been playing on the stairs and had fallen. Blood began to drain into his groin, the pain was excruciating. He tried grimly not to cry out but he could not hold back his anguish.

"Oh, Mother," he cried. "I want to die!"

His sisters gathered about him and tried to give him comfort.

"Have courage, Alexei," Tatiana said. "We will remain with you and will help you. You will soon be better again."

They waited with him along with Doctor Botkin who had travelled with them from Tsarskoe Selo. There was nothing that the doctor could do to relieve the pain. Alexei grew thin and yellow and they feared for his life. Night after night they prayed before their icons for some miracle.

"If Rasputin were here he would cool his fever and Alexei would be well again," Alexandra said.

But Rasputin was dead, his body had been burned and his ashes had blown through the forests. They were alone, far from the centre of things, and there was no one who could help them.

With time Alexei recovered. His pain abated and he began to smile and joke with his sisters. Soon he was well enough to play cards.

Meanwhile in Saint Petersburg the Soviets were now in charge and the upper classes were rounded up and ordered to clear the snow from the streets. The soldiers stood by and insulted them as they worked. All over Russia statues of the Romanov emperors were toppled from their pedestals.

Everywhere committees of Soviets were set up. They would rule the new world and set down new conditions – they would change the world. In the south of Russia, a new army was gathering, soon to be known as the White Army. Would it sweep up to Siberia and save the Imperial family? It was a hope which was secretly entertained by many.

But already there were plans to relocate the Romanov family. The Soviets had grown strong beyond the Urals. Hatred for the family was intense. Rumours began to circulate of great treasures which the family had carried with them.

Captain Karl called to see Vasily one evening. He had not been to the tavern so he was sober. He was also depressed.

"The time for escape is over. The Soviets have taken over Siberia. Now various groups of the Red faction will fight over the family."

"Why?" asked Vasily.

"Some wish to execute them. Others would like them to stand trial in Moscow which has become the capital. Lenin and Trotsky are in charge. Life is cheap at present. The old order is gone for ever."

"What can we do?"

"At this moment, nothing. Watch the house and watch the city. Soon they will come for them. They have already placed a spy in the house. He reads the diaries and he has searched their trunks for jewels."

"How do you know these things?"

"I drink with the soldiers and the Soviets at Ekaterinburg. I hear more than I am expected to hear. They think I am nothing but a drunken bum. I entertain them and sometimes pretend to sleep in their presence."

Captain Karl slipped out of the warehouse at dusk.

That evening Vasily decided to explore the city.

porch. They wept as they said goodbye. Nicholas made the sign of the cross on his daughters' foreheads before turning tearfully away from them. Alexandra did not betray her emotions. The soldiers watched with interest.

They boarded the Siberian carts. Their Doctor Botkin, was to accompany them. He had been with them from the first days of their exile and was always attentive to their needs. He was a retiring man whose quiet presence gave them confidence.

"I will travel with you," Yakovlev said, looking at Nicholas. "You are not wearing an overcoat," he remarked.

"I always wear a topcoat," Nicholas replied.

Yakovlev ordered one of the servants to bring heavier clothes. When they were organised, the horsemen fell into a rough formation.

They moved away from the governor's house and rode through the town. A scouting party proceeded them. Heading south, they crossed rough countryside where the snow had partly melted.

It was a difficult journey. The roads were little more than muddy dirt tracks. Alexandra's body was racked with pain. She had never travelled in this fashion before.

As they passed through the night she feared for the safety of her family and the health of her son. His image would not leave her mind.

Meanwhile, Yakovlev and the Tsar argued about politics. It helped pass the time. Yakovlev was worried that they might be attacked by marauding bands of soldiers.

Finally they arrived at the village of Ievlevo. There, they reined their horses before a large house. It was well prepared and clean, and the soldiers threw a guard about the place.

The owners seemed to recognise the former Tsar and his wife, bowing each time they approached them with food. They gazed intently at all their gestures.

The three Romanovs were so weary after the journey, that they slept soundly through the night. It was cold when they awoke. A thin sun threw shadows across the landscape while a wind blew bitterly from the north. The snow and the rivers were thawing. They resumed their journey through bleak flat lands, broken only by clumps of bare willows and birch.

By evening they reached the town of Pokrovskoe. Nicholas and Alexandra were moved to tears. Rasputin had been born here. On the night of his birth a great meteor had arched across the Siberian sky. They drew up the carriages before Rasputin's house and looked at it. Then they moved on.

Perhaps it was a good omen Nicholas told Maria. The holy man would take care of them.

But Yakovlev was worried. The Uralities, as he called his enemies, were all about him, keeping their distance. He had spotted them on the horizon. They did not attack. Instead, they followed like a pack of wolves as the cavalcade crossed the thawing snow and the wet boggy places.

At intervals they changed the exhausted horses. It grew cold and dark. The detachment moved forward. They reached Tyumen at 9:15 p.m. and a great Siberian moon stood above the town like a disc of bronze.

Yakovlev breathed a sigh of relief. He was exhausted, but exhaustion was a way of life with him.

"Let us get to the train immediately. It will lend us protection," he ordered.

Once on board the train, the whole party were so exhausted they did not even bother to undress. They fell into a deep sleep.

Yakovlev set sharpshooters to guard the train.

"If anyone tries to leave or enter, shoot them," Yakovlev ordered.

He turned to his telegraphist who travelled with him.

"You come with me," he ordered. "We have business to attend to. Bring the codes."

He went to the post office and opened a direct line to Moscow. He sent the coded message which was simple and to the point: "The route remains the old one. Taking Cargo."

Moscow acknowledged receipt of the message.

"Good, Let's move on," he said to the telegraphist.

He believed that he could now outsmart the men from Ekaterinburg. They were a vicious group almost independent of Moscow. They had their own plans for the Tsar and his family.

He boarded the train and ordered it to move forward. It appeared to be moving towards Ekaterinburg, but when the train reached a dividing fork, it switched direction and began to move eastwards towards freedom.

The lights were extinguished and the curtains drawn.

"Where are we going?" someone asked.

"East, it seems. Towards the town of Omsk." A journey of some three hundred miles.

Yakovlev paced the corridor. Had his ploy worked? he asked himself. He had brought the family out of Tobolsk and across the waste lands of Siberia. He had taken them from the teeth of the enemy. He had only to be lucky twice more and they would be saved.

That morning Maria went to the end carriage where the sharpshooters stood.

"Have you any idea where we are going?" she asked.

They nodded their heads. "We are going east," they said. Clearly they were nervous. It was a church holiday and people thronged the train stations. The Royal calvacade moved quickly through them.

Yakovlev paced the carriage like a caged bear.

Late in the night he stopped at a station where he was given some telegrams. When he read them his fury boiled over. "They are going to arrest me at Omsk," he thundered. Perhaps they are on to my plans . . . he thought to himself. He ordered the train to be stopped.

"Uncouple it from the engine," he called.

Then, leaving the family and the sharpshooters on the track, he headed for Omsk in the engine. He knew that he could be facing death, but the challenge excited him.

As he approached the station he began to have doubts. An angry crowd with placards had gathered to meet him. Their anger had been fuelled by rumour and propaganda.

"Yakovlev the traitor. Yakovlev the traitor," they chanted. "Give us Nicholas."

They chanted about him, calling for blood. He knew that crowds acted by instinct.

"I am Special Commissar Yakovlev," he called at the sea of angry faces.

But clearly he clearly made no impression. In the end he was lucky. An old friend arrived to rescued him.

"Quickly, get me to the telegraph office. I have to clear the whole business with Moscow."

"Very well," said his friend. He called a military lorry and they rushed to the telegraph office. Yakovlev discovered that Moscow had changed its mind. Nicholas and his family would remain in Siberia and there was little chance of escape.

"Return to Tyumen immediately. Have come to an agreement with the Uralites," the message read.

Yakovlev knew then that his adventure was finished. His plans had been dashed. He was handing Nicholas and Alexandra over to their executioners. Had they got beyond Omsk, they would have been free. They would have fled east and there lay the ultimate safety.

Yakovlev sent a warning telegram to Moscow:

"If the baggage is taken to Ekaterinburg, then I doubt you will ever be able to drag it out of there."

Yakovlev returned to the station but he did not betray his emotions. He called the train driver and ordered him to travel west to Ekaterinburg. They would not pass through the Urals as Yakovlev had hoped.

From the window Nicholas noted the names of the railway stations. They were going west. Nicholas grew nervous. He paced the corridor, preferring not to alarm his wife and daughter.

He spoke to Yakovlev.

"I wish that we were returning to Saint Petersburg."

"Moscow may change its mind," Yakovlev said.

"But I have read the papers. I know they hate us at Ekaterinburg," Nicholas said with simple honesty. Yakovlev had deep pity for him and wished to save both him and his family, but at that moment the cause seemed lost.

It was morning when they entered the railway station. The station was crowded. News had spread that the Romanov family was about to arrive. Some were curious. Others had come to insult Nicholas and his German wife.

"Bring the Romanovs out and let me spit in their faces. They are the cause of all our trouble," a soldier roared.

"Get out the machine guns and shoot them," another called.

Had the train been close to the platform, they would have pulled open the doors and torn Nicholas and his family limb from limb.

"They behave like dogs," Yakovlev observed.

Maria held herself close to her mother.

"We have not merited all this, Mother. What's wrong? Once these people loved Papa."

"We must bear this suffering with fortitude," Alexandra told her daughter. "Perhaps we have to suffer so that the country should flourish."

The crowd would not disperse. They would have descended on to the tracks but the sharpshooters were ready for them.

The train was moved to the freight depot. Waiting there were three men who would decide what would happen. They were the three leaders of the Ural Soviet and they would control the destiny of the Imperial family. This was the beginning of their moment of glory.

The sharpshooters watched Yakovlev argue with them on the platform. The argument went on for hour and a half.

The three grew tired. They drew their guns.

"We take delivery of the family or we shoot our way in. We have nothing further to discuss with you," they said to Yakovlev.

"Their blood is on your hands," Yakovlev told them.

The sharpshooters were willing to defend the family.

"Surrender your guns," Yakovlev said. "We are surrounded and outnumbered."

The leader of the three moved forward. His name

was Beloborodov. He was young and the revolution was in his blood. He entered the train with a swagger and looked at the Romanovs.

"I will write out a receipt for the baggage," he said in an arrogant voice.

He took a sheet of paper and signed it. Then he handed it to Yakovlev.

"Take it to Moscow. Tell them that the cargo is with us."

"I will take the family to the car," Yakovlev insisted.

"Very well," Beloborodov said.

Yakovlev led Nicholas, Alexandra and Maria to the car. There was no more he could do. Their eyes were sad, almost fatalistic. He waved to them before the car sped away to their new prison. It was called the Ipatiev House and had belonged to an engineer, who had been ordered to vacate it.

They had only a short few months to live.

CHAPTER 13

Vasily stirred in his bed. Light was pouring in through the window. He shook himself and cast aside his blanket and the covering of furs. He went outside and washed at the barrel.

Tobolsk was about its business as always. The blacksmith was shaping iron on his anvil. The sound rang out through the quarter. The baker was delivering fresh bread and the bells were ringing out from the church steeples.

Three days had passed since Nicholas, Alexandra and Maria had departed. In all that time there had been no news of what had happened. Like all the others, he was curious to know the new course of events.

Fedor entered the building.

"Any news?" Vasily asked.

"Yes. I heard it from a friend. They never reached Moscow. They are at Ekaterinburg."

"That is the worst of news," Vasily sighed. "I have heard of the soldiers from Ekaterinburg. They hate the Romanovs. They would shoot them on sight."

"And what is going on at the house?" asked Fedor.

"Nobody knows. I'd better find out."

"How?" asked the furrier incredulously.

"Perhaps through bribes," said Vasily. "It's worth a try."

"You are a smart lad, far advanced for your years. Here take this money." The merchant put his hand in his pocket and handed him several roubles. "See what you can discover. Your friend Captain Karl has sent me a telegram. He is arriving in the next few days. Are the pelts sorted?"

"Sorted and bundled as you can see. We have enough for one cargo," Vasily assured him.

He put on his fur cap and left the warehouse. He noted that the river had thawed during the night and shards of ice were passing down to a distant sea.

Vasily went into one of the many shops on the main street and purchased two bottles of vodka and several packets of tobacco.

He considered the situation. The past year had made him tough. He had studied the soldiers and their leaders with a detached eye. They were ruthless men. The fall of the Tsar had given them power and position. They were the new kings. They swaggered around Tobolsk like small tyrants, brandishing guns and pasting posters on walls. Many of them could not read.

He approached the fence surrounding the governor's house. A soldier pointed his rifle at him.

"Why do you approach this house? Have you business here?"

"I am curious. Who is in charge of the Romanov family?"

"That is none of your business. I have orders to shoot if necessary."

"I see that you smoke," Vasily said.

"When I can afford to smoke. I have not been paid for two weeks."

"Then here is some tobacco," he said, taking a wad of tobacco from his pocket.

The soldier's eyes brightened.

"You are a true comrade. We all call ourselves comrades now but I have noticed that there are those who give orders and look down upon the rest of us as if we were dirt. You ask who is in charge?" he said filling his pipe with tobacco. "Well, it is Commissar Rodionov. He is a malicious snake."

"And his men?"

"Like their master. I'm from Yalta. You know where Yalta is?"

"Yes," said Vasily. "It is on the shores of the Black Sea."

"Smart lad," said the soldier. "I worked there in the vineyards before I got caught up in this war. Someday I will return to the vineyards. The Tsar and his family are simple people. I often saw them in Yalta. But I have to obey my orders."

"Is it possible to enter the house?"

"No. There is no way you can enter the house unless you are the baker or the butcher."

"If I return with food for the pantry, will you let me through?"

"Yes, but each time I let you through I will require a wad of tobacco."

"Very well."

Vasily returned to Tobolsk's main street and found the baker who supplied the house with bread.

"Let me carry it to the kitchen at the governor's house," he said. "I will pay you for your trouble."

"How much?" the baker asked.

"Two roubles."

"Are you a spy?"

"No. I write for a paper in Saint Petersburg."

"You are very young to write for a paper. Write something for me. Here is some paper. Write for me about my bakery. Prove to me that you are a writer."

Vasily sat down. In fifteen minutes he had written three hundred clear words. He handed them to the baker.

"That is very good. I will give you the job, but be careful. These soldiers are nasty men; none worse than Rodionov."

Vasily did not fear Rodionov. He passed through Tobolsk with his basket of bread. He approached the sentry from Yalta, and handed him the tobacco.

"Ah. A new baker's boy. Pass through."

Vasily had penetrated the barrier. He knew the layout of the house. It was well guarded. There was no weakness. It would take a small army to rescue the three young women and the boy.

He arrived at the back door. The servant opened it.

She recognised him.

"You again! You turn up like a bad penny."

"I have brought the bread. I work for the baker."

She looked anxious. Her face was strained and furrowed.

As she began to remove the bread from the basket, she began to whisper.

"This Rodionov is terrible. He is a tyrant and never rests. His mind is dark, even strange. He searches everyone, even the priest and the nuns when they come to pray. And at night time it is worse . . ." When the bread was all out she replaced it and began to take it out again so that she could continue with her story.

"What do you mean?"

"Rodionov insists that the girls keep their doors

open at night time. He has burst in upon them when they are half-dressed. When an old servant protested to him, he waved a pistol in her face."

"That is terrible," Vasily said.

"And the soldiers leer at the girls, making obscene remarks when they visit the toilet." She had the bread half unpacked when there was the thunder of military boots on the stairs. Suddenly Rodionov appeared. He looked suspiciously at Vasily.

"Who are you?"

"The baker's boy."

"Come here, lad," Rodionov ordered. "Put up your hands."

Rodionov searched him and discovered the tobacco in his pocket and the bottle of vodka.

"You drink and smoke then?" he asked.

"It is for my Uncle Pavel. My father was killed in the war."

Rodionov looked at him suspiciously.

"Very well."

He examined the food.

"Make sure they receive their rations and no more. "

"What of the young Alexei? He is weak, and needs nourishment," the servant asked.

"He remains on rations," Rodionov said sternly. There was no mercy in his eyes or in his voice. He turned and thundered back up the stairs.

"He is bloody-minded," said Vasily under his breath.

"Is there any chance of escape?" the servant asked.

"It may be too late. But I will keep you informed."

"You are a good lad."

He left the kitchen and as he passed through the yard he memorised the positions of the soldiers. There was no way that armed men could take the stockade and the house. Vasily hated the governor's house. It was like an island prison. He wondered how Alexei was and if he had enough food for his dog.

That night, as he set down his thoughts, he suddenly felt inexplicably lonely, though he could not say why. He wished he were back in Saint Petersburg with Dimitri and his friends in the printing works. He thought of his mother and her short, hard life, and of his father who had died in the war.

He looked towards the governor's house. Lights were on in the upper rooms.

The next day he worked on the pelts. By now he could sort them by size and quality. Then he bundled them and placed labels upon them. Fedor examined his work.

"You are invaluable to me. Will you stay on in Tobolsk? My family will take you in. You will have heat and comfort."

"It is very good of you, but I must follow this story. I believe it is important that I write my account."

Vasily told him that he had gained entrance to the house. He explained the conditions to him.

"It is terrible. If they treat the daughters of the Tsar in such a fashion, they deserve to be put up against the wall and shot. No decent man behaves in such a fashion."

When Fedor had gone, Vasily continued with his work. He noticed that it had suddenly grown very warm in Tobolsk. The rivers were free and the flowers were in full force. There was a true breath of life in the air.

A day later Vasily returned to the baker's shop. A delivery of bread was ready for the prisoners. He collected the basket and passed through the streets. As he walked he heard rumours. "Is it true?" he questioned a priest. "Are the Archbishop and others going to march on the house with the parishioners and try to free the prisoners?"

"Yes. The Archbishop Hermogen has already condemned the soldiers. Now he will make an attempt to rescue the prisoners. If the numbers are great enough, it may succeed."

Vasily checked the story again. It was obviously true. He wondered if it would work. He could only live in hope.

When he reached the first picket, the soldier from Yalta was there. He handed him a wad of tobacco.

"Any news?" he asked.

"Alexei grows stronger each day. Soon they will be moved to Ekaterinburg."

"And Rodionov?"

"He continues to abuse them. He has pointed a gun at them several times and told them that he has orders to shoot, but the girls have stood up to him. Now, move along, I must not be seen talking to you."

Vasily hurried to the kitchen. As he did so he noted Alexei sitting in a corner of the yard catching the sun. His sister Olga was beside him and his little dog, Joy, sat on his lap. He looked tired and undernourished.

"Ah Vasily," he said, recognising the new baker's boy at once. "How are you? Some day you will take me in the train. I will stand with you in the engine room and we will drive all through Russia."

Vasily was about to answer him but a soldier came forward and ordered Vasily away with the butt of his gun.

"Do you wish to be put in prison? You have no right to approach the prisoners."

Vasily walked in the direction of the kitchen. The

Royal family were obviously starving. The scanty rations were taking a toll on their health.

He entered the kitchen. He could see from the table that there no provisions in the place.

"I have not enough vegetables to make soup for Alexei. He needs his strength built up," the servant said.

"I have brought meat. I was at the butcher's and I purchased it. It should give him strength."

The servant kissed the parcel of meat which Vasily handed her.

"You are a kind lad. What news do you bring?"

"Good news. I believe that Archbishop Hermogen is going to march on the house with his parishioners. They will try to help you escape."

"I do not care for my life. I care only for the children."

Just then a surly-faced soldier entered the kitchen.

"You have done your business here. Move along now."

He had hard eyes and a prominent chin.

Vasily took his basket and left the kitchen. As he passed across the yard, the small dog leaped from Alexei's lap and ran to him. Vasily knelt town and began to pat him on the head.

Instantly the guard was upon him. He butted him with his gun in the ribs, knocking him over. Vasily felt a sharp pain. The small dog rushed away in fear. Vasily looked at the soldier, who was pointing his gun at him before dragging himself to his feet and left.

That night Vasily reflected on what had happened. His side still smarted from the blow and a heavy weight burdened his heart. He could see little chance of an escape from the terrible prison.

The next day Vasily took his gun and walked in the

forests. He had much to think about. Should he walk in the procession? Should he carry his pistol with him? If he were discovered he would be shot.

He felt lonely. He wished his mother were alive. She would have been delighted with his success. He returned to the warehouse and he was surprised to see Captain Karl waiting for him.

"Ah, my young friend. How have you survived the winter? You have a healthy complexion. They must be feeding you well. You have grown. Come with me to the end of the pier. I wish to show you my ship. It is painted and looks like new."

Vasily could tell that he wished to speak with him privately.

They walked out through the warehouse door and into the intense sunshine.

"It's unnatural weather," Captain Karl said. When they were out of earshot he continued. "Soon the steamer *Rouss* will arrive. They are going to take the rest of the family to Ekaterinburg."

"What news do you bring with you from Ekaterinburg?"

"Only the worst. Nicholas, Alexandra and Maria were handed over at the station like baggage and have been confined to the Ipatiev House. I fear the worst. The Ural communists are the scum of the earth."

"There is going to be an attempt to save the family here."

Vasily explained what had been planned.

"It might work. If they are taken to Ekaterinburg, they are finished."

They looked across the wide stretch of water, so peaceful under the sun. There scent of flowers was in the air and a gently breeze lifted from the river.

"I know the captain of the *Rouss*. He is a friend of mine," Captain Karl told Vasily.

"Can I find a berth on board?" Vasily asked. "I am determined to follow the story to the very end."

"It can be arranged, but you will live a dangerous life. They have spies, known as Cheka, everywhere. At this very moment eyes are following our every move."

Captain Karl and Vasily returned to the warehouse and talked well into the night. The town fell silent. Sometimes the sound of a drunkard singing broke the stillness.

"There may be one more chance of escape but I can say nothing about it at the moment. Leave it at that. The less you know the better," Captain Karl said getting up to leave.

When the pelts were loaded and Captain Karl set sail for Tyumen.

The following day was the day of the procession. The sun was exceptionally hot that morning. Even the moist road began to crack. By midday the heat was merciless. It beat down upon the group which gathered at the church. Once assembled, the procession made its way along the scorching streets. The old people began to drift away. Soon only the Archbishop and a few others remained. Then the Cheka moved. Vasily watched as they bundled the Archbishop down an alleyway followed them.

What happened next was to haunt him for the rest of his life.

They led the Archbishop to the end of the pier. They lay him on the ground and bound him with ropes. Then they took old iron gratings and tied them to his body.

"Hurry," one of them called a boatman.

The Archbishop was thrown aboard and they pushed out into the river. Vasily watched as it swung into the main stream.

A little downriver they lifted the body on to the gunnel and pushed it into the river. There was a short cry which carried across the water. Then silence.

Vasily watched them return. He studied each one as they clambered on to the pier, laughing to each other.

"If they get rid of an archbishop so easily," Vasily said to himself, "they can get rid of a family without compunction."

Clearly the decencies of life were no longer observed. These men were murderers. He watched them pass – they showed no remorse and could have been out for a walk in the forest.

That night, as he passed through the town, a voice called him. It was the sentry off duty.

"Give me some tobacco and I will give you some information," he said.

"What is it?" Vasily asked, pulling the wad of tobacco from his pocket.

"The day after tomorrow they depart. They will be taken by river steamer to Tyumen. Then they will be taken by train to Ekaterinburg."

"Thanks," said Vasily. "I will see you again."

"Perhaps," said the sentry. "Nothing is certain these days."

That night the family gathered in Alexei's room. They talked of the summers they had spent sailing in the Gulf of Finland in their father's yacht. They had picnicked on pleasant islands and had played with the sailors. They wondered if they would ever sail in the Gulf of Finland again.

CHAPTER 14

Vasily watched from his window. The sentry had been correct. The steamer *Rouss* turned in midstream, then eased its way close to the pier. The sailors cast ropes which arched through the air. They were caught by the pier hands and the steamer was secured.

It was time for Vasily to leave Tobolsk. It had become a lonely place. He packed his few books and the large notebooks in which he had written his thoughts. These he placed in a leather satchel he had made from pig's hide.

He entered Fedor's office.

"So, it is time for you to leave. I will miss you. If you decide to remain, I will triple your salary and you can come and live with me as a son," he offered.

"Forgive me, but I cannot accept your generous offer. However, I will always recall your hospitality."

"You will follow the Romanovs?"

"Yes. To the bitter end."

"I hope the end will not be bitter," Fedor said. "I have something for you," the furrier said, going to the safe and opening it. He took out a large wad of money.

"This is for you. You may need it at Ekaterinburg."

"I cannot accept such a sum." Vasily looked shocked. He had never seen such a huge amount of money in his life.

"Take it. You will find good use for it. It may help the family."

"Very well then. Thank you," said Vasily, tucking the roubles inside his shirt.

Fedor paused. "I will write a letter for you, so that you can get a job in Ekaterinburg. I believe Captain Karl has made arrangements with the captain of the *Rouss*."

"Yes."

"I will be at the pier when you leave."

Vasily bundled his belongings into a large sack, slung it across his back and walked down the pier. Some soldiers were guarding the ship. They raised their guns as he approached.

"Nobody is permitted to board this ship."

"I am a new crew member. My name is Vasily. Ask the captain."

The captain came on deck. He wore a grey pointed beard and was tall and angular.

"Come here," he directed.

Vasily walked up the gangplank with his bundle.

"You see this deck? I want you to scrub it. Last lad I had was useless. Every ship should sparkle."

The soldiers were impressed by the roughness of the captain's voice.

Vasily found a mop and bucket and set to work. While he was working, the first lorryload of Romanov suitcases arrived on the pier. They had come from the governor's house.

They were carried on board and placed on the deck.

"They can sort their own luggage," one of the soldiers said to the captain. "We are no longer serfs."

Then they reversed the truck along the pier, swung it about and set off for the heart of town.

Vasily looked at Tobolsk. It appeared beautiful under the bright sun. The golden onion-shaped domes glistened in the sunshine. Beneath one lay the jewels of the Romanovs – only two people knew of their location. The white walls glowed and the town itself looked charming. Trees in bloom softened the outlines of the houses. Many coloured flowers grew in the window boxes. Women in summer frocks hung out the washing. Life was pleasant and the air was light.

On the river itself men cast nets from shallow boats. They called to each other across the water.

"Come here." The captain's voice broke Vasily's reverie.

Vasily followed him into the cabin.

"Can you use a revolver?" he asked directly.

"Yes. I have practised in the wood. I carry one with me but I am not always accurate."

"If you need to use a revolver, it will be at close range. I may have to call on you. You can return to the deck now." He said nothing more, but looked stoically ahead.

Vasily wondered what the captain had in mind. Would there be an attempt to rescue the family? Vasily had much to think about as he returned to his work.

Vasily listened to the conversation of the men. They were edgy.

"Keep your eyes keen. There is always the chance that someone will try to rescue them at the last minute. There are spies in town. They may choose this moment to move."

"I wish we were shut of them."

"We will leave that to our superiors."

"Everybody is equal now."

"Tell that to Rodionov."

Silence fell between them. The lorry returned with more suitcases which were hauled on board.

"That's it," the driver said. "Next time we bring the human baggage."

Vasily waited. He hoped that something might happen. Perhaps friends were preparing to rescue them. This would be the ideal moment – when the soldiers were exposed.

Then the trucks arrived bristling with guards. They surrounded the prisoners and their retainers. They pushed them up the gangplank. Almost immediately Rodionov ordered the ropes to be slipped and the anchor to be hauled in.

Black smoke belched from the funnels as the boilers were charged with coal. There was a dull sound from the horn at the steamer moved out into the river. It began to move south away from the town.

Vasily turned to the deck. Alexei was there with his little dog Joy. Beside him stood his three sisters like guards. They were dressed in similar white dresses and had grown thin and pale during the winter.

His eyes met Alexei's. They recognised each other.

"Come here," the captain called him. "Show the girls to their cabin. Hurry up, you lazy whelp. I'll teach you to work!"

Vasily rushed forward.

"Follow me," he told the girls. The former Grand Duchesses followed him into the best cabins. They were clean and neat and smelt of fresh linen.

"The captain is a friend," Vasily said.

"I recognise you," Tatiana said. "You were in the train which took us here and you brought bread to the kitchen."

"Yes, that's right. I hope to be of service to you. I've brought some chocolate. It is from a friend in Tobolsk. It is hidden beneath your pillows. Now I must say goodbye for the moment." With that he left the cabin.

"Come here," the captain called again. Vasily rushed to his side. He caught him by the ear.

"Do you understand Russian?" he roared.

"I do, sir, I do."

"Louder!"

"Yes, sir. I do."

"Then show this young man his cabin. I am putting you in charge of this baggage. Do you understand? They are your responsibility!"

"Yes, sir. I am in charge of the cabins, sir."

"And you keep them clean and scrub them out and wash the portholes and keep the brass shining. Do you understand?"

"Yes, captain."

"Well then, get about your business," he roared, pushing him forward.

Vasily threw himself on the ground with a dramatic gesture before standing up.

The guards began to laugh. It was a perfect situation. Vasily had become the ship's fool.

"Follow me," he told Alexei. He brought him to his cabin.

"I am sorry that you were humiliated before the soldiers. It was quite horrible. The captain is a cruel man."

"He is a friend," Vasily whispered. "It was an act."

"Well, you fooled me," Alexei told him.

Vasily returned to the deck.

"Come here," a voice called. It was Rodionov. "I recognise you from somewhere."

"Yes sir. I worked for the baker. He was a terrible master. I ran away today. The captain needed a cabin boy."

"Search him," Rodionov ordered.

The soldiers frisked Vasily for weapons.

"He is clean," they said.

"Remember, everyone is a suspect," Rodionov warned them. He surveyed the remainder of the people who stood sheepishly on deck.

"Find your own accommodation. This is not a palace. If there are not enough cabins, sleep on deck. The journey will soon be over," he told the retainers.

He called the captain.

"You," he said roughly. "Make sure that the doors to the women's cabins are open at all times."

"Even at night time?" the captain asked incredulously.

"Yes. It is at night time that plots are hatched. The boy's room remains shut. Understand?"

"Understood," the captain said. A nerve vibrated in his neck.

The guards began to drink cheap vodka. Soon they were lolling about the deck shooting at passing birds. Each time they brought one down, they cheered.

One had the idea of setting up a machine gun. Soon it was chattering horribly, spent cartridges falling about the deck.

"They are in a dangerous mood," Vasily said to the captain.

"So I see. I will teach that gunner a lesson tonight."

The soldiers now turned their attention on the three sisters, who sat on deck chairs at the front of the boat.

"Which would you like for a soldier's wife?" they asked a raw recruit with black teeth.

"The young one," he said.

"She is too fat. You think she could milk a cow? Or keep you warm at night time? Better an ordinary woman from your village than one of the Royal Duchesses."

Anastasia was terribly conscious of her weight. Despite the bad food at Tobolsk, she was still plump.

"What about the oldest one?" the machine gunner asked. He had a malicious smile on his face. "I doubt that she would soil her hands in a hay shed forking out dung. No, she was not reared to anything like that. Better a village woman."

Tatiana stood up. Though she was taller than the machine gunner, she stared at him in the eye. "You are very brave when you are in the presence of defenceless women. I wonder if you would be as brave facing your enemy? I have nursed those brave men in my home at Tsarskoe Selo. I have washed their wounds and have helped to amputate their limbs."

For a moment he stared at her in fury before drawing his revolver. He would have shot Tatiana but for the steel hand of the captain which grasped his wrist. He squeezed it until the machine gunner cried out in pain, letting the revolver drop on to the deck.

"There will be no blood shed on board my ship," the captain said. "Is that clear?"

Rodionov arrived on the scene. The captain turned on him.

"You must control your men on board my ship," he ordered. "If not, you can sail it yourself."

"You challenge the authority of the state?" Rodionov answered. "They will hear of this in Moscow."

Rodionov gathered his men about him and gave them some orders. They returned to their positions.

Vasily went down to the galley. He asked the cook to prepare some soup which he carried to Alexei's room. Alexei was alone, lying on a bunk looking wistfully out the porthole at the river. Joy lay at his side.

His eyes opened with delight when Vasily entered.

"Welcome! I have had no company. My sisters are taking the sun above on deck."

"I've brought you some soup. It is good for you. How are you feeling?"

"The pains will not go away. They are terrible but I have learned to bear them. Sometimes at night I cannot sleep. But today they have eased. Look."

He lifted his white shirt and showed Vasily a large purple spot on his leg.

"I bleed inside. There is no cure for it. But tell me of your adventures. They must be very varied. Have you seen many interesting things?"

"I have learned how to drive a lorry in Tobolsk," Vasily said.

"Is it difficult?"

"Not when you get the hang of it. And I know how to maintain the engine."

"How wonderful. Tell me more."

Vasily sat beside his bunk and told him of his adventures. Alexei looked at him in wide-eyed wonder.

"I wish I had been with you in the forests, or in the engine room of the train."

"Perhaps some day we will go on a great adventure together," said Vasily.

"I do not know. Father will not be Tsar again and I

have no right to the throne. I do hope that I won't always be a prisoner though." Alexei looked sad.

They talked for quite a long time. As Vasily talked, he shone the brasses.

Suddenly Rodionov appeared.

"You have spent a long time here. Anything the matter?"

"No, the place was filthy and I had to clean it. These are my orders. The captain is a terrible tyrant. He will beat me if everything is not spick and span."

Grumbling, Rodionov left.

"He is a nasty man," Alexei said. "He lacks manners. He has treated my sisters in a most ungracious way."

By now Alexei had cheered up. He stood in the cabin and walked up and down.

"You have put me in a good mood," Alexei said.

Then Tatiana entered. At first her face was sad but when she saw how happy Alexei was, she cheered up.

"You are walking again, Alexei," she exclaimed.

"Yes. My friend Vasily brought me some food and has told me of his adventures in the forests. He has led a most exciting life."

She looked at Vasily. Tears of gratitude shone in her eyes.

"I am most grateful to you," she said. "We have had few friends who could help us. What age are you?"

"Fourteen, going on fifteen," said Vasily proudly.

"You are very tall and strong for your age. How long have you been in Tobolsk?"

"I have been with you ever since you left Tsarskoe Selo. If I can help in any way, I will. Now you must excuse me."

At that moment he knew that he would die rather

than let anyone harm them. He had seen both sides and knew who the demons were.

Vasily spent the rest of the day working about the ship. He visited the engine room and spoke with the engineer who explained how the complex pistons worked. In the evening he watched the sun going down behind the flat lands. As night descended the soldiers began to drink again in small groups. Their voices grew louder and they began to argue amongst themselves.

Vasily listened to their querulous words. They were about to attack the Grand Duchesses.

"We will have them dance for us," one roared.

"Yes, let them dance like the gypsy girls."

The captain emerged from the shadows holding a revolver.

"The first one to move will be blasted from the face of the earth," he said.

"You defy the people's army!" one soldier said.

"And you are a rabble," he told them. They were about to descend upon him when Rodionov appeared.

"What's the matter now?" he demanded.

"The captain has called us a rabble. We wish to see the women dance."

"Return to your watch," Rodionov told them. "Tomorrow they will be delivered at Tyumen to the Ekaterinburg Soviets. They will deal with them. It will be out of our hands."

"They should die," the machine gunner called.

"Yes," they said. "Let them die now. Let's get rid of them. They have blood on their hands."

"Even without a trial?" the captain asked.

"They are symbols of the old regime. They should die without a trial!"

"Is their no justice in this new republic?" the captain asked.

"They should die," they said.

"Return to your posts," Rodionov ordered. He had become worried, not for the family, but for his own life.

His orders were clear. He must hand over the prisoners alive.

The night was crisp and clear, the stars bright in the sky. The engine grumbled while the propeller threshed the water beneath the bow.

Vasily heard the captain's voice. He looked about and could barely make him out against the darkness.

"Come with me," he whispered. "Here are some cigarettes. I wish you to offer them to the machine gunner. He is by himself at his post."

Vasily was about to question the captain but refrained.

He moved forward towards the machine gun position.

"Who goes there?" he gunner asked drunkenly.

"I have come with some cigarettes," Vasily said.

"Who told you to bring them?"

"A friend."

The gunner rose from his position. Vasily offered him the cigarettes.

What happened next was swift and lethal. The captain emerged from the darkness. He put his hand around the machine gunner's mouth. With a swift plunge of a dagger the machine gunner was dead. The captain held him firmly, then pushed him overboard where he disappeared without a trace in the wake of the roaring waters.

"He was the worst of them; he had a miserable

heart. Say nothing about what you have seen. Good night."

Vasily returned to his bunk and tried to sleep. But the bulging eyes of the murdered man would haunt him forever.

The sun rose, turning the sky into white silver. The breeze was pleasant and carried the early scents of a summer morning. The great Siberian world was beginning to wake and fall into the ritual of summer.

Vasily paced the ship deck. They had some hours to travel before they reached Tyumen. He looked at the deserted machine gun post. There was no stain of blood on the deck.

The soldiers were confused. They asked one another if they had seen their friend. Did he call out in the night? Was he below deck drunk? They searched everywhere for him.

"He must have fallen overboard," the captain said. "It has been known to happen."

His voice was factual.

But for some reason or other the soldiers were quiet. At the back of their minds they felt that something unfortunate had happened him. Perhaps there was an assassin on board.

The whole Royal suite crowded on deck and chatted pleasantly with each other. Perhaps the fact that they were moving up river gave them a sense that they were returning to normality.

Vasily had time to bring some food to Alexei in the morning. He played with the little dog as he ate.

"What will happen us now?" Alexei asked.

"I do not know. You will be taken to Ekaterinburg to join your parents."

"What type of place is Ekaterinburg? Are there palaces there?"

"I do not know," replied Vasily.

"You know that normally at this time of year we would be at the Livadia Palace in the Crimea. It is very beautiful. We were always happy there."

"Perhaps you will find your way back there some day."

"Perhaps. I will send you a special invitation if I do — you will be my guest."

When Alexei had finished the bowl of soup, Vasily took it and returned to the galley.

"You seem sad today," the cook said.

"I am. They do not deserve to die."

"What do you mean?" the cook asked.

"Nothing," Vasily sighed and he returned to his small cabin. For the first time in a long time he wept.

It was midday when they docked at Tyumen. Immediately the steamer was surrounded by soldiers. As always they were bad-mannered and brusque.

They lined up the passengers. Alexei looked weak and uncertain. Vasily rushed to him.

"Put your arm about my shoulder," he said.

The young boy put his arm about Vasily's neck and helped him trudge forward some distance to the waiting train. There, he helped him into the second-class compartment with his sisters and some close attendants. The rest were placed in the fourth-class car.

"Are you one of them?" a soldier snarled.

"I am a ship hand. I've come to help."

"Let them help themselves."

He heard the small dog bark. Joy had been left behind in the confusion. He ran to Vasily who gathered him in his arms and carried him to the carriage.

"Your dog," he said simply.

The little dog ran to the boy and jumped into Alexei's arms.

"Thank you," Alexei said.

The doors of the train were slammed shut. Steam issued from beneath the engine in a soft cloud. The wheels began to turn slowly. The soldiers pulled back.

Vasily watched the train move out of the station. Soon it passed around a bend and disappeared.

CHAPTER 15

The Urals run like a long wedge from north to south across Russia. Ekaterinburg was situated on a cluster of low hills on the eastern slope of these mountains. In winter the streets were a quagmire thick with mud and snow. In summer they were dry and dusty. Ekaterinburg lay on the railway networks and had a telegraph line directly to Moscow. Spires and cupolas rose above the roof tops. The buildings in the centre of the city were elegant and finely proportioned.

In 1918 Ekaterinburg was run by the Soviets. They had set up their own system of law. Despite its distance from Moscow, it kept in direct communication with the capital.

The train carrying the remainder of the Royal family arrived in the city on the night of 22 May. A slight drizzle was falling. The naked lights about the station were blurred by the fine rain.

Immediately soldiers threw a cordon about the train. The prisoners looked out through fogged windows at the grey station.

"What is happening?" Alexei asked.

"I do not know, but soon we will be with Mother and Father," Tatiana told him.

A smile brightened his face.

"We will be all together again. That is wonderful."

Later a grey light filled the sky. The buildings looked drab and deserted. It was only much later that people began to appear. An old heavyset woman with a wide face and a broom cleaned the platform. She stopped to watch the Royal family's train as it passed, before continuing to sweep up the dust and litter.

Later, some passengers arrived and waited for a train at a further platform. Tatiana felt jealous of their freedom as she watched them through the window. She wondered what lay in store for them. She wondered what the new house would be like. Would they enjoy freedom to walk about? Would birds sing in the trees and would they be able to dig the garden and plant seedlings?

If only they could return to the Livadia Palace far to the south, with its peace and tranquillity, they would live there forever and let some new ruler govern Russia. Her father had never wished to be tsar. Some soldiers appeared with droskies: low-wheeled carriages, with tops. The soldiers threw open the second class carriage.

"Out! Out!" they yelled.

"What of our bags?" Olga asked.

"You are well fit to carry them yourselves. We no longer have servants in Russia," the soldier glibly replied.

The Grand Duchesses descended from the train with their bags. The rain had turned the dust to mud. It sucked at their feet as they trudged forward with their suitcases.

A servant took Alexei and carried him to the drosky. Then he returned to help the Grand Duchesses.

"Where are you going?" one of the soldiers asked.

"To help the young women . . . "

His face met a rifle butt and he fell backwards into the mud.

"They are fit to take care of themselves," the soldier sneered. "Rabble," spat the servant.

Immediately the soldier pointed the rifle at his head. "Lives are cheap at present. Hold your tongue."

The servant dragged himself to his feet. He felt humiliated by the peasant in uniform.

Finally their luggage was aboard the droskies and they set off for the Ipatiev House, situated on a hill above the city. They studied the streets and buildings as they passed through.

Then they climbed the hill. The Ipatiev House came into view. A tall barrier of stakes had been set up about it and it was only when they entered that could see it properly, glistening with whitewash.

Immediately Nicholas and Maria rushed out to greet the new arrivals. They threw their arms about each other and wept openly.

"Alexei seems to be well again," Nicholas said, looking at his son. The small dog barked at his heels.

"Come and see Mother. She is not well at the moment. She has so looked forward to meeting you."

They rushed indoors and up to the first storey which had been set aside for them.

The Ipatiev House belonged to a retired army engineer, who had acquired it a few months earlier. It was a two-storeyed stone house with a long façade. He had purchased it because it possessed hot running water and electric lights. The upper storey had been furnished. It consisted of three bedrooms, a dining room, bathroom and toilet and other facilities. Beneath the house lay an empty basement.

Everywhere guards were posted; at the fences, in the attics, and at all corners of the building.

Meanwhile, at the station, the family retainers remained in the carriage. They were beginning to grow anxious. They had noted the behaviour of the soldiers and listened to their insults. Ekaterinburg was a hostile place. They were far from Saint Petersburg and the quiet isolation of Tsarskoe Selo. They had not followed the vicious logic of the revolution. Now they began to fear for their safety. Suddenly Rodionov began to bang on the doors of the carriages.

"Get out! Everyone out! Take your luggage!"

The retinue clambered down from the train and walked across the muddy ground to the droskies. Led by the head of the Red Urals, Alexander Beloborodov, the procession passed through Ekaterinburg to quarters some distance from the Ipatiev House.

Beloborodov was a jolly, blue-eyed young man of twenty-seven. His appearance belied his intent. Five of the retainers were picked from the lot. They were taken to the local prison.

Of the five one would escape with his life.

Those not taken to the prison would soon be asked to leave the province. They would carry the story of all that had happened with them to cities as far-flung as Saint Petersburg and Moscow.

The Romanov family had finally been isolated. Like the governor's house, the Ipatiev House was like an island prison. Life flowed past, never intruding upon it. The executioners were gathering at Ekaterinburg. Plans were shaping in their minds.

CHAPTER 16

Back in Tyumen, Vasily boarded a train. In his sailor's bag he carried his notebooks, some rough clothes and his copy of Pushkin. He looked out at the station. It was a vast place with tangled rail lines of which he could make little sense. A few old women carrying baskets entered the carriage. Even on hot days they wore heavy black clothes as if they were in mourning.

Three soldiers entered the compartment carrying rifles. They took out their pipes and began to smoke. Now and then they spat on the floor. Soon the carriage was filled with the smell of coarse tobacco. The train began to move into flat open country.

"There is trouble further east," one of the soldiers said.

"We have no enemies to the east."

"Some Czechoslovakians have taken over the railway further to the east. They have been working in Russia when the war broke out. Now they have formed a foreign legion."

"Are you certain?"

"Yes."

"Are our lines to the east cut?"

"Yes."

"I hope we are not dragged into it. I'm returning home to attend to my farm."

They began to talk about land. With the revolution they had obtained small farms from the Soviets.

"I feel like a king every time I look across the waving grass. No more masters for me. I'm a free man."

"Unless we are called into another war," the other replied.

They spoke of farming for most of the journey, discussing seeds and cattle and how to build a proper house on their newly acquired land.

They got off at a nondescript station along with the two old ladies. New passengers came on board. Vasily kept looking through the windows at the eternal plains of Siberia, now green and fresh in the summer heat.

He fell asleep as they passed into the foothills of the Urals and by the time he awoke they had reached Ekaterinburg.

He stepped out of the train and looked around the station.

Before long he found himself wandering through the town. It was a hilly place unlike Tobolsk. The streets were wide and many of the buildings lavish and well built. Several church steeples and domes broke the skyline.

Vasily made his way to the address given him by Fedor. It was a huge general store containing innumerable goods. He was surprised at their quality. At the back was a huge timber yard where planks stood in great blocks.

He handed the owner, Mr Bazulin, a letter. He was an old man with runny eyes. He read it carefully.

"Fedor speaks highly of you," he commented. "I owe him a favour. I will give you work. However, you must find your own lodgings. Come back tomorrow and I will start you in the timber yard. It is hard work but I can see you are a strong lad."

Vasily disliked him. There was something mean in his eyes. It was obvious that the workers in the shop were afraid of their master. Vasily swung his bag on to his shoulder and began to make his way through the town. It did not take him long to discover where the Romanovs were imprisoned.

He made his way up the streets to Ascension Square. A magnificent church stood in the centre. Across the road stood the Ipatiev House with a palisade of raw timber about it. Only the upper windows and attic rooms could be seen from the distance.

They are certainly afraid of something, Vasily said to himself. The security was not as intense in Tobolsk.

He noted the presence of soldiers stationed about the house. They carried revolvers and hand grenades. He moved towards one of the guards.

"Good day, Comrade," he began.

The soldier looked at him. "Where are you from?"

"Tobolsk. I worked there during the winter. Now I am in Ekaterinburg. I am looking for cheap lodgings. I will pay five roubles a day."

He could see the guard calculating in his mind.

"Go to my wife. She will put you up. We have a small room."

He gave Vasily his address. The youth made his way to the poorer quarter of the city and knocked on the door of a small cabin. A heavy-set young woman came to the door. A small unwashed child held her skirt and looked up at him.

"Your husband sent me. He said you would have lodgings here."

"How much are you willing to pay?"

"Five roubles a day."

"You must be prepared to pay a week in advance."

"Very well," said Vasily.

He put down his bag and took some notes from his pocket. He handed her thirty-five roubles.

"How long will you be staying?"

"A week. Perhaps more."

"Come in."

He followed her into the cabin. It was a filthy place which smelt of boiled cabbage and sweat. His room was a lean-to at the back of the house with a small window and a torn curtain. There was a table under the window and an iron bed against one wall.

"It will do," he said.

"What are you doing here?"

"I have a job with the timber merchant, Bazulin."

"He is an enemy of the people. Some day he will be shot."

"Who said so?"

"My husband, Misha. He hears everything." With that she left the doorway which she had blocked with her heavy presence.

Vasily set his few possessions on the bed, put his money in a pouch he carried around his neck and left the hovel. He took a deep breath of fresh air, before making his way up to the high hill on which the Ipatiev House was built. He surveyed it carefully.

It was almost impregnable. There were machine gun emplacements on every corner. He would have to wait his chance. Perhaps he could gain access. But it seemed impossible. He wandered through the city; it was late when he returned. By now Misha had returned with one of his friends. They had been paid and they were drinking with Larissa, Mischa's fat wife. The child was asleep on the cot.

"Come here," the soldier said. "Have a drink with us."

"I don't drink," Vasily told him.

"Then you are not a Russian. You know who was behind the fence today?"

"Who?"

"Nicholas. I was guarding Nicholas and his family. He is a nobody. The commander Avdeyev will rub his face in the dirt, let me tell you. Mister Romanov is a citizen now. A citizen like me and you. And you know something?" he said, bending towards Vasily and dragging him on to a chair. "The women have to ask permission to go to the latrines. Now isn't that something? The Grand Duchesses have to ask permission from the common man when they want to relieve themselves. And while they are at it, the guard stands outside the door."

The two men and the sloppy woman burst out laughing.

Vasily felt revolted. He restrained an impulse to take the vodka bottle and smash it on the soldier's head.

The child began to roar in the cradle.

"Can you not keep the brat quiet?" Misha roared in Larissa's direction. "Can my friend and I not have some peace?" She picked up the child and rocked it in her arms.

"Have you heard of the jewels?" Misha whispered.

"No," Vasily leaned forward conspiratorially.

"They have jewels worth a fortune but no one can find them. They must be in the house. But where? That is the question."

For a moment Vasily swallowed. He remembered the

night that he and the priest had hidden the satchel of jewels in Tobolsk. He wondered if there were further treasures.

"Tell us more," the visitor said.

"After another drink. There is much to tell."

Misha poured out a tumbler of vodka and gulped it back. Then he continued talking.

"The recent arrivals slept on mattresses on the floor the first night."

He began to laugh.

"I'm sure they once slept in beds of gold studded with diamonds," Larissa said.

"And the young whelp of a prince hurt himself. They say he has a blood disease. It runs in the family," Misha said.

"Death also runs in the family. Nicholas is fifty. He won't live to be fifty-one," his friend said.

"Is this true?" the woman still nursing the child asked.

"There are plans but I can say nothing more. My lips are sealed. The man to watch is Yurovsky. He is dangerous."

"Yurovsky?" Vasily repeated.

"Yurovsky."

"Who is Yurovsky?" Vasily asked.

"He's the local photographer," Larissa said. "He took my photograph once."

"And did the camera explode?" the husband chuckled.

"Go away," she said laughing.

"But this Yurovsky?" Vasily continued.

"He is as smooth as silk. He is planning something. He says nothing but he is behind the scenes. Moscow knows what's going on. The telegraph wires are humming between Ekaterinburg and Moscow. Coded messages. Did you ever see a coded message?"

"No," Vasily lied.

"It's all numbers. The numbers are letters. Those in Moscow can change them into words. I talk too much. I'll sing instead."

Misha began to sing. He sang in a raw voice about love. Halfway through he slipped to the floor and fell asleep.

"Throw a blanket on him. Let him sleep it off," Larissa said. "It is time for bed."

Vasily began to piece together the situation. He had learned much from the conversation.

All the signs were ominous. Had the Romanov family taken their chances in Tobolsk, they might have escaped; now they were in a fortress, surrounded by people who hated them.

Vasily began work in the timber yard. It was strenuous, but it gave him a base in the city and money to sustain himself.

Each evening he climbed up the hill to Ascension Square. He walked about the palisades looking for some weakness, but he could find none.

Inside the building life was oppressive. The heat was intense and the Imperial family were not permitted to open windows. They remained in stuffy rooms, while guards marched up and down the corridors. The windows had been painted and only dim light filtered through. The family could not so much as move from room to room without permission, and were not permitted to take exercise in the yard. They knew that a summer breeze blew down from the Urals and that it would be refreshing to walk in the confined strip between the house and the palisades outside.

They read to each other. Nicholas began to read *War and Peace* – a vast book which engaged his mind.

The family knew the nights on which the soldiers got paid. They could hear them singing in the cellar close to where their luggage had been stored. On such nights their minds were filled with dread. The guards might rampage through their quarters and even rape the Duchesses. They were capable of anything.

The Imperial family found peace and solace in prayers. Each day was punctuated by prayer. They had carried their most sacred icons with them which they arranged on the walls of their rooms. Their guardian spirits would protect them. Life was constrained and boring.

One evening Alexandra said "The commander is searching for the jewels. They know we have hidden them somewhere."

"They will never find them, mother," Tatiana told her.

"Already the soldiers are pilfering from our luggage. The last time I visited the cellar, I noted that some framed photographs were missing, along with other items."

"Why not complain to Avdeyev?" Olga asked.

Nicholas interrupted. "I detest that man. He is a boor. He leers at us. He is a disappointed little man. Not much better than those ignorant guards. I have heard what they have said to the girls. It is grossly insulting,"

Tatiana moved forward. Had she been Tsarina, the empire would never have fallen.

"Father, we are women now. You forget that we are

responsible people. We will retain our resolve; we will not weaken."

"I wish I'd had councillors about me with your courage when I needed them. Let us hold firm," Nicholas said.

Alexei had been confined to bed. A fall on the stairs had opened some internal wound. He wept at times when he could not sleep and sometimes wished that he were dead.

Each day his father carried him to a seat in the sunshine. There he lay, thin and wan, trying to draw health from the Siberian sun.

Despite the coarse manner of the guards, many of them were impressed by the quiet dignity of the Royal family and their ability to adjust to their simple environment.

Olga grew closer to her mother and became introverted. She read her books and prayed before the icons. She felt at the back of her mind that they would soon be killed and believed that they would never leave the house alive or return to the delightful climate of the Crimea.

She had written out a prayer in her own hand which displayed this attitude. She was preparing for some dark end.

Vasily hated his work at the timber yard. One day, as he passed a garage, he decided to ask the owner for work. There were several automobiles and lorries in the city and he had often listened to their purring engines as they trundled past.

"Well," the owner asked. "What can I do for you? You don't own an automobile or a lorry in need of repair, do you?"

"No, but I would like to work here. I have worked with machines before."

"Can you drive a truck?"

"Yes. I learned in Tobolsk."

"Good. I will employ you, but remember, I cannot afford to pay you a high wage. Times are bad, but I need a keen lad. The army need their lorries serviced."

"Thank you. I'll take the job. I have had enough of the timber merchant. He is a tyrant."

"Pytor, the mechanic, will show you what to do. He is stripping down the engine of a lorry. Go over and help him."

Pytor was a humorous man with a wooden leg.

"You see this wooden leg?" he said. "It saved my life."

"How did it save your life?" Vasily asked. "Did you knock somebody on the head?"

"No," Pytor laughed. "When the war came the sergeant major looked at my leg and told me that I was a useless fellow and of no use to my fatherland. So I was dismissed and returned to the garage. All I want to do is fix machines; they are wonderful things. One day I will build an automobile and drive in style through Ekaterinburg!"

While he talked he began loosening screws. He handed Vasily a screwdriver.

"Many hands make light work," he said.

They worked in the garage all day. The engine was hauled out of the bonnet by a pulley and carried to a bench where it glistened with oil.

"I will have to strip it down. A piston shaft is broken. Lucky the machine didn't explode."

Vasily followed every movement as the engine was taken apart and each section laid out neatly on the bench.

"What did I tell you, a broken piston shaft!" Pytor said, lifting out the damaged part.

It took them two further days to replace the engine in the lorry. It was put together piece by piece. By the time it was finished Vasily had a good idea of how the whole system worked.

That evening Pytor backed the lorry out of the garage and they went for a test drive. They passed through the town and drove up to Ascension Square and then out along the road to Koptyaki village about fifteen miles from Ekaterinburg.

Beyond a level crossing they passed through some dense forest. Some peasants were coming towards them on the road with their carts. They quickly drew aside.

"That's power," Pytor smiled. "Now you try."

Vasily's experience had been limited in Tobolsk. He climbed into the driver's seat and moved forward, cautiously changing the gears to gain experience. Then he accelerated. He was delighted at the power of the lorry and drove all the way to the edge of the city.

"Better give it to me," Pytor said. "You don't want to kill somebody on your first day out."

Later Vasily said goodbye to his friend and returned to his lodgings. He had been there for a week and detested the stench, the perpetual drinking and the confined space.

He entered his small room by a back door.

"You," a voice called. "Come out here. Join your comrades."

He had no wish to join them but it was at night that he often discovered what had happened at the Ipatiev House during the day.

Misha was bleary-eyed.

"Can you sing?" he demanded.

"No," Vasily lied.

"Well then. Can you play the mouth organ?"

"No," Vasily lied again.

"You can't sing and you can't play the mouth organ. What good are you to your country?"

There was white foam at the edge of his mouth. He looked like a dog with rabies.

"Last night the Grand Duchesses played for us. They played "Let's Forget the Old Regime" and lots of other tunes. You see, I can sing and I taught the songs to them. We woke them up in their shifts and got them to play. We are the masters now. Isn't that right, mate," he said to his friend.

"Yes, mate, we're masters and have roubles in our pockets and boots on our feet."

"And children that don't sleep," Larissa said when the child began to roar.

"Speak well of the child. He is a son of the new order."

Vasily wondered how the guard could drink so much vodka.

"We have plans. Lots of plans for the prisoners. When the birds fly south, the hunter shoots them. Bang." There was a twisted smile on his face.

When Vasily finally got to bed, he lay awake and tried to put the pieces of the jigsaw together.

Clearly something was going on in Ekaterinburg of which he had no knowledge.

He liked his work in the garage, particularly his friendship with Pytor. Pytor was a good teacher and had fine fingers. He could find a fault with an engine and fix it immediately.

"Watch the boss," Pytor told Vasily. "He is a friend of the Secret Police. That gives him power. He is one of

the Reds, but he is afraid. I have been listening at
keyholes and I overhear things."

"What is happening?"

"The Cossacks are coming."

"What Cossacks?"

"The Cossacks from the east. They are sweeping
across Siberia. I tell you the Reds are growing afraid."

"Then there is a chance that the family may be
rescued?"

"Keep your fingers crossed."

Vasily's mind was filled with expectation. But he did
not know that a larger game was in play. Moscow was
threatened; armies were massing all over Russia,
threatening the position of Lenin and the Reds.

Far away in Moscow, sitting at his desk in the
Kremlin, Lenin was hatching plans. Each day military
reports were brought to him in the great fortress. The
Red armies were drawing back.

He remembered many things. He remembered how
his brother had been hanged by the Romanovs and
how he himself had had to flee into exile because of
the Royal family. The family would be wiped out, trunk
and branches.

He began to make preparations with the Red leaders
at Ekaterinburg.

The Imperial family and its immediate relations must
all be wiped out.

They should be killed on a journey or trying to
escape. It was a good idea.

Vasily did not know this as he passed through the
town on the ninth of June. It was a pleasant evening,
the light lingered on the horizon. As he was passing the
main street, he noted a detachment of men mounted on
horses followed by some trucks moving east.

"What is happening?" he asked somebody.

"Some of the detachments are changing over to the Whites."

"I don't believe it," Vasily gasped.

"Judge for yourself. They believe that the Reds will be defeated and wish to be on the winning side."

There was consternation in the city. For the first time he noted fear in the Red soldiers' voices.

When he went to bed that night there was no singing in the kitchen. Instead, Misha and his wife were whispering over the table. They were sober and mistrustful.

"Have you heard any more rumours?" they had Vasily asked when he had entered.

"Apparently some of the detachments have moved over to the Whites," Vasily replied.

"What about the guards on the Ipatiev House?"

"They are still there. "

"Good."

He couldn't sleep. He was excited. Perhaps the palisade would be pulled down? Perhaps the Romanovs would be set free? He asked himself many questions before falling asleep.

The next day the town was unsettled. People began to move out of the small streets and challenge the Red presence. Vasily watched their faces filled with determination. There were young people with fresh complexions, soldiers who had been to the Front, peasants who laboured in the fields and yards, old women with heavy hips, round faces and coloured scarves. And amongst them everywhere were agitators, goading them on. They chanted as they moved forward. Vasily kept close but out of sight. They moved along the main street and up the hill. They gathered at

Ascension Square where they became a dense threatening mass shaking their banners and placards in the air.

The guards at the outer rim of the Ipatiev House, withdrew close to the palisade. They looked fearfully at each other.

Vasily watched. Yurovsky looked unsure. It was the first time that Vasily had seen him close up. He possessed a tight narrow face. His eyes flamed with anger as he rallied his troops, forming a long line. They moved towards the crowd and fired into the air.

The crowd refused to move. Then Yurovsky signalled the machine gunners set on the roof of the Ipatiev House, who fired a round of ammunition above their heads. The bullets knocked fragments from the wall of the Cathedral,

The crowd began to break apart. Soon it dispersed into small groups which began to disappear down the main road of the city. The square lay empty.

The final attempt to save the Tsar and his family had collapsed and Vasily felt depressed as he made his way towards his miserable lodgings.

CHAPTER 17

"It is time to kill them," Yurovsky told his companions. They had gathered in Room 3 of the Hotel America. It was a luxurious place, once been the preserve of the rich merchants of Ekaterinburg. Furs, timber and wheat had been traded here. Precious stones had been spread out on green baize. Great meals served on the polished tables. Now the Reds had taken over.

"Take them out and shoot them, just as Michael, Nicholas's brother, was killed," Markov advised.

"Explain how the execution was planned," Yurovsky directed.

"It was very simple. He was living in a hotel in Perm with his British secretary, Brian Johnson. Some of our friends walked into the hotel, grabbed Michael by the collar and dragged him out on to the street. Johnson followed. They threw them into a drosky and set off for the forest. They shot Johnson in the head. When Prince Michael tried to comfort him, they blasted him too. They buried them the next day. Markov was one of the executioners. Lenin received him at the Kremlin. He told the story to the great man himself," Markov said directly as if explaining a practical matter.

"Lenin hates the Romanovs. He would be delighted if we got rid of them all. His brother was hanged by one of the tsars," Yurovsky said.

The conversation gave them a certain amount of confidence. But underneath, they were afraid. The enemy was advancing. As they looked at the map, they knew that soon the Whites would throw a circle about Ekaterinburg. They discussed their position.

"Then let's murder them. Make the preparations," Yurovsky directed.

"Better to shoot them en route. Pretend that they tried to escape. Better still, we could say their supporters attacked us and they were caught in the cross fire," one suggested.

"Will Moscow agree?" Yurovsky asked.

They wired Moscow. A day later they received a coded reply. They were not to make any move.

"But why?" one asked.

"Lenin may want to use them as pawns. Perhaps the Germans wish to do some deal. After all, Alexandra is related to the German Kaiser," Yurovsky explained.

They were all uneasy. Within weeks they could be standing before a firing squad. Soon they would have to leave Ekaterinburg. There was no way they could hold out.

By now Vasily had worked out the key figures in this terrible game. Vasily listed their names in his note-books. They were all there, each one described in detail.

He decided to move from his lodgings. He had discovered as much as he could and noticed that Misha's friend no longer visited the house.

The woman cursed him when Vasily told her of his decision.

"You should have told me," she said. "I could have had another lodger ready to come in."

"Who would stay in this kip?" Vasily retorted, "it stinks of cabbage and stale sweat and a dirty child with a dirty mother."

"You whelp!" she said taking the brush to attack him. She made a wide useless swipe, tumbled over and fell on the floor.

"That's the end of your vodka money," he said throwing the last of his rent on the floor.

He rushed out of the cabin with his few possessions and up the road. He had sufficient funds to move into more pleasant quarters close to the Ipatiev House.

Vasily continued to work at the garage. He learned how to take an engine apart, fix it and set it to work again. Pytor was a good teacher. He loved his job and when he was not working he liked to fish. Vasily sometimes accompanied him on fishing expeditions.

Behind the palisade their life had become tedious. Each morning they rose early, prayed and had a simple meal. They worked at their sewing and darning. Each weary day was passed in reading or sewing. Sometimes the princesses went to the kitchen and the cook taught them how to make bread. Their laughter filled the kitchen as they threw flour at each other. Despite the continued attention of the guards, they never discovered the jewels. They never realised that they had been sewn into the young women's stays. Alexandra now cut Nicholas's hair. Like her own, it was growing grey. She remembered when both were young; when he was crowned Emperor many years before.

He had been handsome and she had loved Russia then. She still loved the vast country, but she hated those in charge. Had she been with Nicholas, she would not have let him abdicate. The war would have been won. They would be still Tsar and Tsarina.

Despair grew in Nicholas's mind. If only they would let his family go free, he would gladly face the firing squad.

His jailers no longer permitted him to receive the newspapers and he had no idea what was happening in the world beyond the terrible fence.

Then he received a message. It arrived in the mouth of a milk bottle smuggled in by the nuns from a nearby convent. He read it anxiously. It was written in French and stated that a group of friends were preparing to rescue them.

"It is wonderful news!" Alexandra told Nicholas, "Soon we will be free. You must reply to the note."

They established a correspondence through the convent.

The plot began to thicken. Nicholas set out a plan of the rooms.

Yes. Escape was possible. Alexei could be drugged. It would kill the pain which racked his body so that he would not scream as he was being carried out.

Nicholas described the house in detail. It was guarded by fifty men. There was a machine gun both on and under the balcony. There was a bell at each guard post in case of attack.

Everything seemed to be falling into place. During the daytime the heat in the rooms was intense. They found it hard to bear and wished they were free to walk through the open meadows, pick apples in an orchard and run along the garden paths.

They prayed that their deliverance was at hand and waited for a whistle at midnight.

Each evening the family noted the light changing in the room. Each evening darkness came a little earlier. They slipped open the window and waited for the whistle. Night after night they waited. It never came.

The commander got drunk more frequently and hurled abuse and obscenities at them. Their nerves grew taut as night after night he waved a pistol in their faces. He ordered the young princesses to play music for his guards, and he had sat in at meals and deliberately pushed his plate on to Nicholas's shirt. But the former Tsar kept his temper in check. This, too, annoyed the commander. He did not have the final power over them.

Meanwhile all their possessions were being pilfered. Every day something was stolen from the cellar, placed in carts and lorries, and driven away.

Nicholas grew irritated. He complained to the commander.

"You accuse us of stealing?" he roared. "We do not steal. We merely repossess what belongs to the people."

"You are no gentleman," Nicholas told him.

The commander closed his fist and shook it in Nicholas's face.

"You watch your tongue, citizen Nicholas Romanov. I have power not only over you but over your daughters, so your ignorant thoughts to yourself."

In room 3 at Hotel America the Red leaders sneered.

"They have fallen into our trap. They believe that our letters are from a friend and have committed themselves to flight. Let them run free. Shoot them as they run."

They laughed at Nicholas' family's simplicity.

"He fell for the trick, hook line and sinker," Yurovsky told them. "They idea of using the convent was perfect."

"So the letters are not real?" one of the communists asked.

"Of course not. We forged them. Now we know exactly what is going on in Nicholas's mind. We keep a close note of his diaries."

"Will he die?"

"Of course he will die and so will the others. They are symbols, and symbols must be destroyed. You have seen what has happened to the statues."

But their composure was soon shattered. An officer entered the room. He had come from the battle front and his uniform was dusty and torn. His head was bandaged. He went straight to a map and pointed to their position beyond the Urals.

"Each day we lose ground. We cannot hold them back forever. They have taken our positions."

"How long can we hold out?"

"We need reinforcements from Moscow or Saint Petersburg. Without them we are finished."

They looked at each other. During the last fifteen months, since the imprisonment of the Tsar, the new empire had been baptised in blood. Lenin had become the new tsar. Now everything was collapsing around them.

"Soon we will have to make a decision to kill the family," Yurovsky said. "I must clear everything with Moscow. I will move into the house with some hand-picked men. We cannot trust the others. They are boors and thieves."

Yurovsky had been a watch-maker. He possessed a keen, exacting mind and concealed his feelings.

"And what will you do?" Medvedev asked.

"Lead them into a false sense of security. Keep a sharp eye on things and discover where the jewels are hidden," Yurovsky replied.

In early July the commander was fired. Yurovsky abused him in front of the Royal family. He called him a drunken lout and a thief. Some of the head members of the Communist Party were there when it happened.

"Out," Yurovsky shouted at him. "You have made a mess of this place. You deserve to sleep with dogs."

The soldiers collected their equipment and slouched out of the place.

New guards were installed in the house. Tall and surly, they were clearly not Russians. They were well trained, said little and set about their business of guarding the house. They were of various nationalities: German, Hungarian and Ukrainian. They belonged to the Communist Party and were cold-blooded killers.

That evening Yurovsky arrived with his assistant Nikulin, a tidy young man with a clean side-buttoned shirt. He did not drink and could be relied upon.

Yurovsky itemised all the Romanov jewellery and gold possessions he could find. They were placed in a box and returned to the family.

"I will lock the shed where your luggage is stored," he told the family. "Nothing else will be stolen from you."

Life became ordered and pleasant once again. Nicholas and his family no longer feared the arrival of drunken boors who would burst into their rooms or order them to play the piano. No longer would obscenities be hurled at them. They liked the new order. Yurovsky lived in the house during the day. Nikulin was there at night.

Pytor and Vasily were working at the back of the garage one evening when Sergei Lyukhanov arrived. He was a short man with a beak-like nose and a spotty face. He drove a lorry which belonged to the secret police.

"Pytor," he called. "It needs an overhaul."

"Very well, Sergei. When do you require it?"

"In the next few days. The oil needs changing and it needs a new set of tyres. And check the engine."

"These look good enough," Pytor said, studying the tyres.

"Not for what they will be needed for."

Sergei looked at Vasily. "Can he drive a truck?"

"Yes."

"Can he keep his mouth closed?" he asked Pytor.

"Yes."

"Then I will need him in a few days' time."

With that he left.

"Who is he?" Vasily asked.

"He is the best driver in Ekaterinburg. He works for the secret police. So keep your mouth closed."

Two days later Sergei Lyukhanov returned. He examined the lorry with a professional eye. He started the engine and revved it up to its highest pitch, nodding his head in approval.

"Did you change the plugs?"

"I did."

"Send the bill to the spies' headquarters."

"Now, lad, come with me."

Vasily jumped in beside him. He noted how he handled the lorry.

Sergei gave him a watch. It was shaped like half an egg and was made of gold.

"I want you to time a run for me," he told him as they drove up the hill to Ascension Square.

He moved the lorry to the side of the Ipatiev House. He turned off the engine. Then he started it again. "Now," he shouted. "Check your watch." He revved the engine hard until the lorry vibrated.

Then he sped away. Past the British Consulate down the hill, past the lake and out the road to the west. They drove across the first level crossing and then the second by the Station hut.

It had been raining and the lorry's wheels found it difficult to find purchase in the ground. Sergei shifted the gears and forced it out of a rut.

"Damn these dirt paths," he said. "They are treacherous."

He continued along the path. Then they stopped.

"Now, let us walk," he said.

They emerged from the lorry and walked through the forest path until they came to the shafts of some disused mines. Sergei picked up a few rocks and threw them into the mouths of the mines, counting how long it took for them to reach the water.

He walked about muttering to himself. His actions were those of a mime artist. He seemed to drag invisible bodies along the ground and push them into the mines. Then took an imagined hand-grenade from his pocked and threw it down the mine.

Afterwards they returned to the lorry, backed it up and returned it to the garage.

"How long did all that take?" he asked.

"Two hours."

"Good. That should do. Wash off the dirt from the lorry. I will return tomorrow."

Vasily told Pytor what had happened. He laughed as he explained Lyukhanov's antics.

"He's up to something. He's no fool." Pytor told him.

That night as he walked home, it suddenly struck Vasily what he had witnessed. At that moment he knew that the Romanovs would not leave the Ipatiev House alive.

CHAPTER 18

High in the Urals lightning flashed and forked and the thunder rumbled like the cannon of some distant battle.

The lightning flashes were frequent during that summer. With it came heavy rain. The rivers ran thick with muddy water and the dirt tracks and mud roads became almost impassable.

After the rains the air was filled with the rich scent of flowers. The Imperial family would have dearly loved to walk in the fields or plant a small garden. But summer wore on and they felt more and more isolated from the outside world. Nicholas did not know at that moment that he had been abandoned by his relatives. The Kaiser in Berlin and the British Royal family in London would offer no asylum.

Despite their hardships the family never lost heart. They were always full of laughter and even the stolid guards sometimes laughed. The small dog Joy was everywhere; he ran along the corridor, in and out of his master's bedroom and barked cheekily at the guards.

On 12 July the Romanov family noted that workmen

were hoisting heavy railings in front of their window and secured them. The bars formed a sinister cross on the opaque window, a constant reminder of their lack of freedom.

In the east, the White Army was fighting its way towards Ekaterinburg. Already the gold reserves, which the Reds had acquired, had been removed from the bank in Ekaterinburg and taken to Moscow. The archives of the party had also been removed.

"I do not like this Yurovsky," Tatiana told her mother. "I have watched him. He does not smile and he has a cruel mind. He is not like the last commander. This one is shrewd."

"Always remember to have the corsets ready to wear. If we escape we must carry the jewels with us. We will need them abroad," their mother told them.

"But will we ever travel abroad? Every day our lives get more isolated."

"Do not let the other girls or Alexei hear you speak like that. Pray before the icons that we will be delivered from this terrible place."

Alexandra was now confined to bed. Her back was wracked with pain. Beside her bed stood the wheelchair in which Nicholas often pushed her about the first storey.

"At least they have permitted us to have religious services. That gives us hope," Tatiana remarked. She looked at the window. The top part had not been painted and she could see that there was a blue Siberian sky.

And as they talked of their condition, a train was arriving from Moscow. The head of the Ekaterinburg communists, Goloshchekin, was on board. In his briefcase he carried the death warrant for the Romanov family. It had been approved by Lenin. He had sat with the bald-headed revolutionary in his office in the Kremlin. Lenin had spoken of his childhood, of his imprisonment in Siberia, of his years wandering in Europe.

"Execute them as soon as possible. We might have brought them to Moscow and had a show trial, but we have no time for that. Let the deed be done in Ekaterinburg before the White armies arrive. Cover your traces. I want them destroyed."

He took a sheet of notepaper and signed it.

"Contact me by telegram as soon as the executions are finished. You will be remembered forever for this service. You have served the party well."

The train entered Ekaterinburg Station where an official car was waiting to collect Goloshchekin. It sped out of the station and headed for the Hotel America.

The Ural Executive Committee was waiting for the final decision from Moscow.

"I leave it in your hands Yurovsky. You know what is expected of you," Goloshchekin said.

Yurovsky showed no flicker of excitement. His eyes were impenetrable, his face intent.

"It will be done. Certain preparations will have to be made. The executioners are already in place."

"Have they been informed?"

"No, but they will obey my orders." With these words Yurovsky left the Hotel America and immediately called on Sergei Lyukhanov.

"Have you found the site?" he asked.

"Yes. It is at a place called The Four Brothers."

"That is a peculiar name."

"It is called after four pines which grow from the same trunk."

"Let us go and examine it."

They walked as far as the garage. Vasily saw them approach. He could sense how serious and tense Yurovsky was. He watched as they climbed into the truck and backed it out of the garage.

"We will be back in two hours," Lyukhanov told Vasily. "The lorry will need to be checked again."

Was this the moment? Vasily asked himself. The truck returned three hours later. The wheels were thick with mud. Yurovsky was in a vile mood.

"You think you could make that journey at night, even under wet conditions?" Yurovsky asked..

"Yes, sir. You can trust Sergei Lyukhanov."

Sergei remained for some time in the garage. His boots and trousers were stained with mud. He cursed Yurovsky.

When he left, Vasily checked the meter. He knew that they had been in the Four Brothers mining area again.

"I will stay late and check the lorry," Vasily told Pytor.

When Pytor left, he closed the garage and switched on the naked lights.

He drove the lorry over the pit and stood beneath it. He studied it very carefully. A thought crossed his mind as he looked up at the chassis. It was risky but he was willing to take the chance. He took three thick ropes and secured them to the chassis. He tested them well for he would have to depend on them. Then he put out the lights and made his way home. He decided to walk up to Ascension Hill. He looked at the rough palisade set about the house and wondered how Alexei and his dog were.

That night Nicholas wrote the last entry in his diary:

Alexei, his son, had taken his first bath since his arrival from Tobolsk. His knee, which had been very sore, was improving but he could not bend it completely. The weather was warm and pleasant. He had received no news from the outside world. With these few thoughts, he half-filled a page of his diary which he had kept for over forty years.

As Vasily studied the house, troops marched up the hill and east. They followed a military band. They were Red supporters and they were about to engage the White army which was advancing on Ekaterinburg. In a matter of days they could take the town.

That night Vasily wrote up his report in his notebooks. Each month he had sent one to Dimitri in Saint Petersburg. He looked at the night sky before he went to bed. Tongues of lightning flashed, ripping the sky into jagged pieces. The air was filled with the pungent smell of sulphur. Then there was a deluge of rain.

Vasily tossed and turned the whole night.

The next day was Sunday. He woke early, ate a simple breakfast and walked up towards Ascension Square. It was ten o'clock. As he stood and looked at the house, he noted two priests making their way to the entrance. He was surprised.

Once inside the house, the priests entered Yurovsky's room, an unkempt place littered with hand-grenades and bombs. Yurovsky was drinking tea. He studied the priests. One appeared to have difficulty breathing.

"What is wrong with you?" he asked.

"I am ill with pleurisy. I have shortness of breath."

"Then you should take care of yourself. I studied medicine once."

While the priest put on his robes, Yurovsky gave him medical advice. When the priests were ready, they moved into the family quarters. Father Storozhev studied the family carefully. Young Alexei was sitting in the wheelchair. He looked pale and sickly. His mother was dressed in lilac, one of her favourite colours. She had grown old and her eyes were suspicious.

The former Tsar was dressed like a Russian soldier, in a field shirt, khaki trousers and boots.

He noticed that the girls' hair had grown and reached to their shoulders. They were dressed in white blouses and dark skirts. As always, he was impressed by their dignity and beauty.

The ceremony began. When Father Storozhev commenced the prayer, "May the souls of the dead rest in peace with the saints", the deacon beside him began to sing. All the family fell to their knees. It was a strange gesture.

When it was over, the priests left the room and disrobed in Yurovsky's office.

On their way home the deacon turned to Father Storozhev and said, "Do you know, something has happened to them."

"Yes. They are all somehow different and none of them sang."

Much later Vasily contacted the deacon. He asked him what had gone on in the Ipatiev House.

"Why should I tell you?" the deacon had asked.

"Because I have followed them since their captivity. Everywhere they have been I have been close to them. Tsarskoe Selo, Tobolsk . . ."

"Very well, I will tell you," and with that he explained what had happened.

"And Yurovsky?" Vasily asked.

"Yurovsky enquired after Father Storozhev's health. He was interested in medical matters. He was drinking tea. He does not believe in religion."

Vasily left. He knew what was going on in Yurovsky's mind. He was letting the family have the final rites. He was playing upon their religious beliefs. He was wooing them into a false sense of comfort. Their martyrdom was close at hand. Of this Vasily was certain. But where would Yurovsky murder them? In the house? In the forest? How would he get rid of the bodies? Vasily thought of the mine shafts he had seen with Sergei.

Monday the 15th arrived. Alexandra continued to keep her diary. She described the morning as greyish. Later the sun burst through. That day women came and cleaned the floors. The family read to each other and Alexei had a bath. They played cards and then retired at a quarter past ten.

It had been a day like many other days: confined and dreary. That night she heard gunfire.

In the morning the women came to wash the rooms. When they were about to leave, Yurovsky called them back.

"Wash the ground floor and the cellar room," he ordered. "The place is in a mess. I wish to have it tidy."

Yurovsky was working to a plan which was both tidy and exact. That day the executioners met in Yurovsky's room at the Hotel America. They had volunteered for the work.

"You are all here," Yurovsky said, looking at the eleven men who would help him eliminate the family. Many were eager for the task: Nikulin, Ermakov, the two Medvedev brothers and the Latvians. All were revolutionaries and some of them had been in prison. They all belonged to the Communist Party.

"Once they are in the cellar you will be called in. I will find an excuse to bring them there. It is almost below ground level and Sergei Lyukhanov will have the lorry running. That will muffle the sound. I want no confusion. Each one must know his victim. Each one will aim for the heart. That way there will be less blood. No random shooting. It must be swift and it must be exact. Understood?"

"What if they panic and break up?" someone asked.

"That should not happen. If it does, continue to fire at your own target."

Yurovsky's mind was working like clockwork. Everything was falling into place.

"Now who will have the honour of killing the Tsar?" he asked, looking from man to man. "Later you will boast of this deed. Our friends have suffered in the camps. They have called for the death of the Tsar. They have died from torture and exposure. Now at last we can avenge their deaths."

"I have done hard labour," Ermakov told them. None of the others had suffered so much in the revolutionary cause.

"Then you shall have the privilege of shooting the Tsar," Yurovsky said clinically.

He read down through all the soldiers' names and carefully listed out their victims.

"Then we are ready. The password is 'Chimney sweep'."

They began to laugh. Yurovsky remained grim.

"It is necessary to have such a password. The Whites advance on the town. Be prepared. We will meet at the Ipatiev House this evening."

With that the meeting ended. They made their way back to their own quarters. Each knew what was expected of him.

CHAPTER 19

The sun rose early. The sky was bright. Somewhere in the city a bell sounded. It had a deep resonant tone. The air was fresh and cool and the fragrance of the gardens filled the house. Joy barked in a small impish voice. He rushed about the corridor and entered Alexei's room, jumping up on the bed. The family rose at nine o'clock. The muted light poured in through the whitened windows.

After they had dressed, they gathered together and prayed before their icons. It set a seal on the day, binding each to each in a mystical union. Although they usually sang some religious hymns, on this day they did not.

By now few servants remained with them. Doctor Botkin was still present as well as some servants.

Their breakfast was simple: eggs, milk and bread which had been delivered from the convent.

At ten precisely Yurovsky arrived. He was always precise. His eyes were sharp and he missed nothing. With a quick glance he noted that the windows were secure and that nothing was out of place.

"You have permission to walk for half an hour," he

told them. "It is quite beautiful today. The wind is fresh. I have also brought your further supplies of eggs and milk."

He did not betray his feelings. Already Moscow had been told of their intent to murder the family. They were seeking a final sanction from Lenin.

At eleven o'clock, after Yurovsky had gone, Nicholas and the girls went for a walk in the garden. Alexandra and Alexei remained in the house. Alexandra's feet pained her and walking was difficult for her. She wished to spend the day in her room.

The poor diet during the last eighteen months had made the family pale and thin. It had not, however, dampened their good humour.

Outside, Nicholas and the others studied the thin growth in the confined garden. Every fresh leaf or flower enchanted them. Afterwards, when they had returned to their rooms, they began to read. Nicholas was drawing towards the end of *War and Peace*: a splendid book which had absorbed his attention during the dreary hours.

Tatiana read from her Bible. Today she read from the book of the prophet Obadiah. It was one of the shorter books and described the looting and destruction of Jerusalem. It was a dark, prophetic book of deep and stirring music. Then it was time for dinner. At four o'clock they again walked in the garden.

The walk lasted for half an hour. Everywhere they looked they saw guards. There was no way to escape.

At six o'clock, the kitchen boy was called into the presence of Yurovsky.

"Your uncle is ill. You must go and visit him immediately."

The little boy, who had been with the Imperial

family from the beginning, took his clothes and left Ipatiev House.

Supper was at eight. It was a leisurely affair. Towards nine the girls began to drift off to their rooms.

Nicholas and Alexandra sat at a table and played cards. It relaxed them and it was a pleasant way of whiling away the hours before bed.

At half ten Nicholas checked his watch.

"It is time for bed," he told his wife.

Another dull, confined day had come to its close, but they had been allowed out, and that was exceptional.

At eleven o'clock the lights were switched out.

As he drifted off to sleep, Nicholas wondered if this strange liberty had any significance.

For Yurovsky it had been far from a dull and uneventful day. With the mind of a clock-maker he was working out the details which would lead to the final hour.

He knew that this action would place his name squarely in the history books.

Downstairs the room for the execution had been prepared. He had tested the back wall of the cellar room. It was a plaster partition. It would absorb the bullets. He had arranged for the lorry. It would arrive at the house as soon as Moscow confirmed the executions. Then there was the petrol and kerosene which would be required later. The flesh must be destroyed. The corpses must be unrecognisable.

Yurovsky looked at the sun. It hung above the hills. The weather was good but one could never depend upon it. Often a deluge of rain came unexpectedly from cloudbursts in the mountains. Then the streets were turned into quagmires and dirt paths made travel almost impossible. He hoped it would not rain.

He called in the execution squad and checked their revolvers. They were well oiled, evil-looking weapons.

"I must wait for one final order, then we will carry it out," he told them.

"But how will you get the family to stand against the wall? How will you get them to go downstairs at such a late hour?" one of them asked.

"That is my business. It is yours to follow instructions."

Darkness fell. The guards were positioned about the house.

"If they hear shooting, they are not to be surprised," he told the commander.

"Very well, sir. I will inform them."

Finally it was dark. He handed back the revolvers to the firing squad.

"Check them carefully," he said. "I want no mishaps."

They checked the weapons carefully.

It was growing late. The order from Moscow had still not arrived. The family quarters were in darkness.

Vasily waited in the darkness of the garage. The truck had been sent for a final check.

"Make sure that everything is in order. It is most important that no part should fail," Lyukhanov told Pytor. "If it does, then we are all in trouble."

If Vasily wanted evidence that the family were going to be killed, this was it.

Time passed slowly. At last the door swung open and Sergei Lyukhanov appeared.

Immediately Vasily slipped under the truck and secured himself tightly on the trusses.

The truck sparked to life. Lyukhanov revved up the engine before backing out the door and on to the street. Vasily was about eight inches from the ground. He bounced backwards and forwards and from side to side.

He did not know how long they travelled. But the ropes cut into his back and thighs. Then a door creaked open and they were in the yard of the Ipatiev House.

The signal that Yurovsky was expecting had come through from Moscow.

The engine was switched off and Lyukhanov began talking with one of the guards.

"Has anything happened?" he asked.

"Not yet. But when you get the signal, start the engine. Rev it up so that it will kill the sound of gunfire."

Vasily slipped out of the ropes and lay on the damp ground, He listened as he rolled into the darkness. He held his breath. Somebody was talking. He stood in the darkness. They passed close to him and took up their posts at the cellar window as they had been ordered.

Yurovsky had remained with the sharpshooters in the basement since receiving the news from Moscow. When he heard that the truck had arrived, he knew that everything was now in place. He stood up.

"I will go and wake them," he said.

He left the room and hastened up to the family quarters.

He knocked on the doors and sounded the electric bells.

"We must take refuge in the cellars. There is danger of an attack."

In the bedrooms the family and their retainers began to stir.

"Is this really necessary?" Doctor Botkin asked.

"Yes," Yurovsky snapped. He felt tense. Would he be able to hold his nerve? He felt the side of his face twitch.

"Alexandra finds it difficult to walk, you know. Her legs are paining her."

"We will find a chair for her in the cellar," Yurovsky answered coolly.

It took them forty minutes to dress themselves.

In the meantime the firing squad was directed to take up positions in the room opposite the cellar.

When they were finally dressed, Yurovsky looked at each of them. He felt like the Judas goat leading lambs to the slaughter.

"Follow me," he said.

They formed into a rough line and followed him along the corridor and down the stairs. There were eleven people in all, including Doctor Botkin, the cook and two servants. Alexei was tired and his father carried him in his arms; Alexandra walked with difficulty and was helped by her daughters, who also carried small pillows. The girls wore simple dresses and Nicholas was dressed like a common soldier. They passed down the stairs and out into the courtyard. They crossed the courtyard into another building, through a hall and into the cellar.

Yurovsky possessed the eye of a photographer. "We seem to lack space," he said. "Now could you rearrange yourselves? Let me see. We need chairs. Yes that is what we need. It is necessary that I take a photograph."

One of the guards brought chairs. They were neatly arranged. Alexandra sat on a chair close by the window. Olga placed her pillow behind her mother's back. Vasily, who lay in the darkness, could see Alexandra clearly. Her face was severe and her hair was grey. Her eyes were suspicious. Behind her stood three of her daughters, all beautiful, young women. Nicholas stood by their side holding Alexei in his arms.

"You could sit here," Yurovsky indicated to Alexei and Nicholas.

"If you could move as close together as possible, then everything would be perfect," he instructed.

The others moved into place.

"Alexei is not comfortable," Anastasia said. "Let me place my pillow at his elbow."

That done, she stood behind him.

Yurovsky then produced a camera. He set it on a tripod, studied the family and retainers and took the photograph. There was a bright flash.

"Now if you could remain in that position for a minute."

He removed the camera and left it aside.

The doors were opened and the executioners moved directly into the room. Yurovsky's voice changed. He read out a decree of execution. As he did so, the truck roared into life. It was revved to its highest pitch.

Vasily looked on in terror. He could not believe what he was witnessing. He tried to cry out but his voice was choked by hard fear.

The scene would be etched on his memory for ever.

Nicholas appeared to speak.

As he did so the firing began. Yurovsky pulled his gun and fired directly at Nicholas. Others also, disobeying their orders, fired at the Tsar. Later each would boast that they had killed him. Nicholas died instantly. Alexandra and Olga tried to make the sign of the cross. Alexandra was executed halfway through a gesture. It was a difficult execution. With arms pointing through the doors, they fired at the other victims who ran in terror along the wall. Bullets kicked dust from the plaster. As they poured their volleys into the victims, a strange thing happened. The bullets began to ricochet about the room. The victims refused to die and seemed protected by an invisible shield. The girls were still alive and so was Alexei.

The room was now filled with acrid smoke. The girls lay heaped on the floor. They executioners fired at them again and again.

Yurovsky moved towards Alexei and poured three bullets into his body. They tried to use a bayonet on the girls. There was blood everywhere, on the walls and on the floor.

They threw open the doors to clear the air. Close to Vasily the engine died down to a quiet purr. The room was strewn with bloody figures. Vasily was horrified, tears welling up in his eyes. Every detail was etched on his mind. The rough soldiers moved amongst the bodies. They tested their pulses, then threw the limp arms aside. It was obvious that things had not gone as expected.

Now they had to get rid of the bodies. Someone brought sheets into the rooms. These were tied to cart handles. The bodies were thrown on them and carried through the house to the lorry.

"Did you kill them all?" Lyukhanov asked.

"There may be a stir of life in some of them. We will finish them off in the forest."

"We will have to get the job done before daylight. If

the city discovers what we have done, they will turn on us."

Sergei was worried.

"Open the back. We'll throw the bodies on the floor of the lorry."

"It will make a right mess. There will be blood everywhere."

"Well get a tarpaulin somewhere. Hurry up."

Lyukhanov rushed into the store room and returned with a large blanket. He laid it out on the floor.

The Tsar's body was the first to be carried out.

Lyukhanov shone his torch on the face.

"Dead as a doornail," he said callously. "It's a great night."

Now the girls were stretched on the sheets. One of them began to groan and one of the leaders took a bayonet and struck at her. The executioners searched their bodies for jewellery. They stole their watches, rings and bracelets.

They were carried through the house and out into the yard to the lorry where they were thrown like carcasses one on top of the other. When they closed up the back, Vasily rolled under the lorry and secured himself again. He heard someone talk.

It was one of the soldiers.

"I tell you, some of the girls are alive. What will we do?"

"We cannot shoot them here. We will take them into the forest."

"I refuse to kill them. Nicholas, yes, but not the children."

"Get in and let us be on our way."

The truck began to move out of the yard. Vasily had

been with them from their moment of imprisonment. Now he would be with them at their burial.

He could see nothing. The sound of the engine thundered in his ears. The ground was wet and soon his back was caked with mud. The truck bounced along, past the race track, past the Verkh-Isetsk factory and north towards the Koptyaki village.

Now the wheels had to dig into the mud and sometimes his body touched the road. Vasily tried to arch up away from danger.

The truck passed across some rail tracks. This gave Vasily an idea of his position. Soon there would be another set of tracks beside the station cabin. It was attended by an old woman. He had seen her when he made the run with Lyukhanov.

Vasily knew precisely where he was. It was an area of dense forest.

As the lorry moved towards the crossing, it began to sink into the mud. The engine revved up, the gears ground together in an attempt to move forward.

When the lorry stopped, Vasily immediately released himself and crawled into the thicket.

From the thicket Vasily could hear the voice of Lyukhanov, cursing.

Sergei flashed a torchlight on the wheels.

"We will need planks to move it. And water. The radiator is too hot."

"Where can we get planks at this hour of the night?" asked Yurovsky .

"There should be a railway cabin near here somewhere."

They stumbled off into the darkness.

Three guards remained. They began to talk.

"Soon Ekaterinburg will fall to the Whites. We are as good as dead."

"What do you mean?"

"We are party to the assassination."

Then there was a groan in the back of the lorry.

The guard flashed his light into the darkness.

"Two of them are alive. What will we do? Kill them?"

"No," Vasily called out from the darkness. "Help me save them and I will vouch for you in any court."

"Who goes there?" one of the guards asked.

Vasily emerged from the undergrowth.

"You are but a lad," they said.

"Perhaps, but I possess the experience of a man. I was in Saint Petersburg during the revolution. Please help me, hurry."

The decision was made rapidly. They drew down the duck board and two of the bodies were taken from the heap and dragged into the undergrowth.

Vasily recognised Maria and Alexei.

"One of you must come with me," he said.

One of the men volunteered. The others decided to remain with the lorry for the moment and to abandon it once it started into the forest.

Vasily and the soldier moved forward into the darkness. Vasily carried Alexei on his shoulders. The young soldier carried Maria. They continued to push through the undergrowth and soon they were deep in the heart of the forest. They continued walking through the night until light began to appear in the sky. At dawn they reached at a charcoal burner's hut in the forest. It was abandoned.

"We must rest here," Vasily said.

They laid out the two bodies on the floor. Vasily looked at the soldier. He was about twenty-two with a narrow face and a scar on his cheek.

"Are they dead?" the soldier asked.

Vasily studied Maria. She was moaning deeply and unconscious. Alexei's clothes were bloodied. For a moment they thought that he might be dead. Vasily listened to his heart. He could not hear it beat. He drew open his bullet-marked shirt. Something sparkled. A corset he wore beneath the shirt was shredded, a small stream of diamonds ran out.

Immediately Vasily understood why the bullets had ricocheted off the family. He turned to Maria. She had been stabbed in several places. Behind her ear there was a wound and the blood was still running freely.

"What will we do?" the soldier asked.

"We are safe here for the moment. We must wait. I will find some water and clean out the wounds."

They remained in the hut for two days. During that time Maria never regained consciousness.

Alexei slowly recovered but his mind appeared to be shattered. He called out in a frightened voice over and over again.

Two days later Vasily made the journey to Ekaterinburg. He had to pass through dense woods until he reached the railroad. He marked his position by scarring the trees with his knife. It was midday when he reached the city.

The place was in confusion. The White Army was approaching. The Red front had collapsed. Everywhere the story of the assassination of the Royal family was being talked about. He went to his lodgings and collected his things and money. He paid his rent, purchased some food and clothes and made his way along the railway tracks again.

It was very late when he reached the forest. They ate the rough bread he had purchased and drank water from a neighbouring stream.

Then they dressed Alexei in the rough clothes of a peasant and Maria in a summer dress.

"Now what will we do?" the soldier asked.

"You take charge of Maria. You have the jewels and your parents live nearby. Travel by foot and return to your own country."

"And you?"

"Alexei will come with me. His mind is troubled and he needs care."

They remained at the hut for five more days. Once the soldier slipped away to contact his family in Ekaterinburg.

Then on the fifth day the family of the Red soldier arrived from Ekaterinburg with an ungainly cart, packed with their possessions. They were simple, tough people, with little education but with an instinct for survival. They had come from the south originally and now wished to return to a warm climate.

They carried Maria out of the hut and set her on a rough blanket.

Leaving the hut and passed down the dirt track to a road which led south out of the forest.

At a fork in the road Vasily said goodbye. He stood holding Alexei in his arms and watched the peasant cart trundle along the road. He watched until it disappeared.

"It is time for us to leave," he told Alexei.

They took another road, away from Ekaterinburg directly south away from all the horrid memories and the dark mystery of the forest where the rest of the family were buried in a shallow grave covered by railway sleepers.

It was July and the weather was hot. They had a long journey to make across Russia to the printing works in Saint Petersburg.

CHAPTER 20

It was late summer in Saint Petersburg, the month of the White Nights. Light lingered in the sky for twenty-four hours. The evening light was white and coral pink. It gave the great city a mystical quality. They great domes, bulbous and oval, seemed to float on a mist.

The flowers were in full bloom and the nights perfumed. The city stood on the banks of the river Neva and both the river and the canals reflected its great architecture in the mirrored surface of still water.

Two old men stirred in their dacha on the edge of the city. Light poured in through the windows and warmed the wooden floors. Outside the garden was a riot of colour and the runner beans curled about dry sliver birch saplings. Every year on the same day they made the journey. They were very old men and they had lived through most of the century. They had been in the second great war and in the camps in Siberia but they had survived the purges of Stalin.

In easier times they had set up the printing press. Even now they retained an interest in it. There was so much to remember, so much to set down on paper before their generation passed away.

The taxi arrived. They locked the door and made their way down the path. One used a walking stick.

"We have lived too long," the smaller man said.

"No. We have seen the dark clouds pass. We have seen Russia rise out of the ashes."

The car moved slowly down the dirt road. Dry summer dust swirled up behind it.

They followed an old ritual. They passed down the Nevsky Prospect filled with people dressed in summer clothes.

"It is a free city again. The terrible cloud of socialism has been lifted from the people. It is a greater city than Moscow and far more beautiful," the taller man said.

They passed along the canals and later stopped at the square in front of the Winter Palace.

They got out of the cab and walked slowly across the square.

"I know every room in that palace. My father and mother often stood on the balcony and waved to the crowd. It belongs in another world. I see only the past: beautiful women in gorgeous ball gowns swirling down the marble stairs, the guardsmen in their bright uniforms. I can hear the music. I am delighted that it has survived."

They watched the Neva as it flowed confidently towards the sea. Then they looked at the spire of Saint Peter and Paul's.

"Soon they will all rest in the family vaults in the great fort. All of course, except my sister and me. It was all such a long time ago. There are gaps in my memory."

The cab was waiting for them. It drove them to the railway station. When the entered the train, somebody gave them their seats.

The train moved south. They looked out at the wide plains dotted with copses of silver birch. They noticed a church spire suggesting a village. It was long time since they had made the fatal journey across the plain on their way to Siberia.

And then they reached the Station at Pushkin. A group of tourists who had been in the train with them wished to be taken to Saint Catherine's palace.

"Did the Tsar and his family really live at Saint Catherine's palace?" a tourist asked Alexei.

"I can assure you, madame, they did not," Alexei told her in excellent English.

"Are you sure?"

"Quite sure, madame."

The two men walked along the platform. A taxi took them through the town. They passed through the gates and along the path to the front of the Palace.

The place was completely neglected. As always they sat on the seat and recalled the past. Alexei wept.

"The place was so filled with laughter. I remember the laughter more than anything else. Poor Father. He should never have been Tsar. All we ever wished to do was live in the Crimea at the Livadia Palace. Perhaps I should have died with them."

"You should not speak in that manner. You have lived and you have set it all down. Some day it will find its way into print."

"Should we remain silent about the whole matter? Who wishes to resurrect old ghosts?" Alexei said.

"That is your decision."

They walked slowly along some of the choked paths before reaching the pool with the artificial island.

"It is the laughter I remember," Alexei repeated, looking wistfully out at the island. "That is why I come here."

The hours seemed to fly and before long it was time to go. The taxi was waiting for them. They returned to the station and made the journey to Saint Petersburg.

That evening the circle of friends gathered. Every year they followed the same ritual. Vasily welcomed them and then they passed into the garden and greeted Alexei. They spoke of many matters.

At precisely two a.m. they rose and lifted their glasses filled with wine from the Crimea.

"To the Tsar," they called, raising their glasses to Alexei.

It was the morning of 17 July.

The coral light of dawn filled the sky to the east.